Well, it's because I am a witch.

The Ashen Witch ELAINA
A young woman who has achieved the highest rank among mages—that of "witch." Currently enjoying traveling with her instructor, Fran.

©Azure

"Never change, okay, Saya?"

She was a hard worker. Diligent. Kind. She couldn't stand hurting other people. She never lied. She didn't even tell little white lies. She just lived honestly in the moment, and I was dazzled by her.

WANDERING WITCH 9
The Journey of Elaina
CONTENTS

CHAPTER 1 The Giants' Kitchen 001

CHAPTER 2 A Country Girl, a History Addict, and a Potion Dosing 033

CHAPTER 3 The Resurrection Lily That Blooms in Solitude 069

CHAPTER 4 Cinderella 129

CHAPTER 5 Familiars 171

CHAPTER 6 A Country Girl, a History Addict, and the Aroma of Wheat 225

©Azure

WANDERING WITCH
The Journey of Elaina

JOUGI SHIRAISHI

Illustration
AZURE

9

NEW YORK

WANDERING WITCH
The Journey of Elaina

JOUGI SHIRAISHI

Translation by Nicole Wilder
Cover art by Azure

This book is a work of fiction. Names, characters, places, and incidents are the product of the author's imagination or are used fictitiously. Any resemblance to actual events, locales, or persons, living or dead, is coincidental.

MAJO NO TABITABI vol. 9
Copyright © 2019 Jougi Shiraishi
Illustrations copyright © 2019 Azure
All rights reserved.
Original Japanese edition published in 2019 by SB Creative Corp.
This English edition is published by arrangement with SB Creative Corp., Tokyo, in care of Tuttle-Mori Agency, Inc., Tokyo.

English translation © 2022 by Yen Press, LLC

Yen Press, LLC supports the right to free expression and the value of copyright. The purpose of copyright is to encourage writers and artists to produce the creative works that enrich our culture.

The scanning, uploading, and distribution of this book without permission is a theft of the author's intellectual property. If you would like permission to use material from the book (other than for review purposes), please contact the publisher. Thank you for your support of the author's rights.

Yen On
150 West 30th Street, 19th Floor
New York, NY 10001

Visit us at yenpress.com ✷ facebook.com/yenpress ✷ twitter.com/yenpress ✷ yenpress.tumblr.com ✷ instagram.com/yenpress

First Yen On Edition: September 2022
Edited by Yen On Editorial: Payton Campbell
Designed by Yen Press Design: Wendy Chan

Yen On is an imprint of Yen Press, LLC.
The Yen On name and logo are trademarks of Yen Press, LLC.

The publisher is not responsible for websites (or their content) that are not owned by the publisher.

Library of Congress Cataloging-in-Publication Data
Names: Shiraishi, Jougi, author. | Azure, illustrator. | Wilder, Nicole, translator.
Title: Wandering Witch : the journey of Elaina / Jougi Shiraishi ; illustration by Azure ; translation by Nicole Wilder.
Other titles: Majo no tabitabi. English
Description: First Yen On edition. | New York, NY : Yen On, 2021–
Identifiers: LCCN 2019052222 | ISBN 9781975332952 (volume 1 ; trade paperback) | ISBN 9781975309565 (volume 2 ; trade paperback) | ISBN 9781975309589 (volume 3 ; trade paperback) | ISBN 9781975309602 (volume 4 ; trade paperback) | ISBN 9781975309626 (volume 5 ; trade paperback) | ISBN 9781975309640 (volume 6 ; trade paperback) | ISBN 9781975309664 (volume 7 ; trade paperback) | ISBN 9781975309688 (volume 8 ; trade paperback) | ISBN 9781975309701 (volume 9 ; trade paperback)
Subjects: CYAC: Fantasy. | Witches—Fiction. | Voyages and travels—Fiction.
Classification: LCC PZ7.1.S517725 Wan 2020 | DDC [Fic]—dc23
LC record available at https://lccn.loc.gov/2019052222

ISBNs: 978-1-9753-0970-1 (paperback)
978-1-9753-0971-8 (ebook)

10 9 8 7 6 5 4 3 2 1

LSC-C

Printed in the United States of America

CHAPTER 1

The Giants' Kitchen

I am always very direct about my feelings, a characteristic that I think I probably picked up from my teacher, Miss Fran.

I certainly never suggested out loud that I would like to travel together with her, yet there we were, flying on our brooms, heading in the same direction.

The plains below us, mostly flat and empty except for a few small, squat shrubs, seemed to stretch on forever. The green grass below swayed with the wind like ocean waves, as the sound of a refreshing breeze came out of nowhere and blew between and past us.

I wish I could keep flying through this scenery forever.

I turned this thought over in my mind as I listened to the lonely sound of the wind.

"Elaina?"

Just then, Miss Fran spoke up.

She was wearing her usual kind smile.

"Aren't you getting a little hungry? Come to think of it, I haven't eaten anything since this morning. I don't really care what it is, but I'd like to eat something; how about you? Aren't you getting hungry? Shall we take a little break?"

"……"

Miss Fran's inelegant words ruined the moment.

I let out a sigh. "Well, you should be able to find plenty of weeds to eat, don't you think?"

"My, my. You can't be serious about me eating weeds, or anything of the sort. Who do you think I am?"

"My teacher, Miss Fran."

"That's right, I'm your teacher, Miss Fran. And by the way, isn't it true that pupils typically treat their teachers to meals as a show of gratitude?"

"I haven't the faintest idea what you're talking about."

"It's common knowledge."

Mm-hm, sure... This common knowledge *certainly wasn't known to me.*

"Anyway, I'm in the mood to have you treat me to something, Elaina."

"You say some really absurd things when you're in one of your moods…"

But, well, we're together for the first time in a while, so it would be easy enough to treat her to a meal.

"Won't you treat me to something tasty?"

She sure is persistent, this teacher of mine.

With a sigh, I said, "All right," then with a smile, I added, "If I can even find anything edible around here, that is."

We were in the middle of a journey.

There was nothing but grass and trees as far as the eye could see. Even if there was anything to toss into Miss Fran's bottomless pit of a stomach, the only things growing around us were weeds and acorns.

I guess she's requesting a dish of weeds. When did Miss Fran start liking weird food, I wonder?

"Oh-hoh-hoh." Miss Fran laughed at my words and smiled boldly, as if to say she had been waiting for this moment. "You said you would, right? You said you would treat me, didn't you?"

"I did say that, but…"

…But so what?

"Well then, I'd like to take you up on that."

"But, Miss Fran, there's nothing here…"

There's not a cook in the world who works with only grass and flowers and acorns. Even if I wanted to treat her, there was no place to spend my money, and even if I was going to do the cooking, there weren't any proper ingredients.

But Miss Fran, full of confidence, said, "No, no, Elaina, take a good look at your surroundings. There is grass, there are flowers, and there are acorns, right?"

"......"

"That should be plenty."

"......"

When did Miss Fran start liking weird food, I wonder?

"No, no, really, there's a great restaurant just up ahead. Really, there is. Have I ever once lied to you, Elaina? I haven't, have I? Wait, I have...? No, I have no memory of that... I don't think I have? At least, that's not how I remember things. No lies, not from me. Anyway, there really is a tasty restaurant, I'm telling you..."

On and on.

Miss Fran pushed through the small forest, dragging me along behind her. As we proceeded, she kept grabbing flowers, acorns, and weeds from the side of the path and shoving them into my pockets for some reason.

"...I really doubt we'll find a restaurant in a place like this..."

"It's here. I know it is. It's a hidden gem, a real well-kept secret." As she said this, Miss Fran pointed to a spot in the trees farther on. "See, look over there."

"......"

There was, in fact, a cottage, standing right there.

It looked like it had been used as someone's vacation home a long time ago. The wooden walls and roof were falling apart, and I got the impression that it wasn't so much a restaurant as a private residence. That is, if anyone lived there, which seemed unlikely, given the poor state of the place. It looked altogether abandoned.

No matter how I looked at it, it didn't appear to be a restaurant.

However, near the front door, there was a single sign.

It read THE GIANTS' KITCHEN in big block letters.

"……"

I looked at Miss Fran. "Um, is this place…legit?"

"It is. This restaurant operates all year; they never close. Look, the sign says, 'Open for Business' today as always, right?"

"I feel like maybe they should take a day off, though…"

Well, that's not really my problem. What is worrying is the fact that the place looks like it might collapse at any moment. Is this even safe?

"This place is like a little hideaway in the woods."

"More like it's just a house, hidden in the woods."

"Restaurants like this always serve the tastiest food, in contrast to how they appear. That's what it means to be a well-kept secret."

"It looks *too* well kept. I don't see signs of anyone else…"

"But it's always delicious," Miss Fran said as she forcefully pulled me inside. "Well, shall we go in? It really is wonderful, you know. You won't regret this! Come on."

"……"

I had a bad feeling about the place…

○

As we made our way inside, I hoped to myself that perhaps it was only the outside of this restaurant called The Giants' Kitchen that was so run-down, and that the inside might be clean and well kept instead. I was trying to be somewhat optimistic, but I figured that probably wasn't the case.

It was not a surprise to see that the inside was just as dilapidated as the outside. I figured that a restaurant that isn't inclined to keep up the outside isn't likely to keep just the interior in good order.

There wasn't even a proprietor around when we passed through the front door.

Welcome to The Giants' Kitchen. You must be tired. Please remove your footwear.

The front door opened into a small room. The only welcome was these words, carved into the door on the opposite wall.

It was clear that the custom in this restaurant was to remove one's shoes. I had visited a number of countries to date that upheld the same custom, so it didn't bother me. Miss Fran and I both took off our shoes and tossed them into a shoe box that was sitting off to the side.

But when we passed through that door, we didn't see the restaurant, just a wall with some hangers on it.

Your clothing may get dirty during your stay. Please leave any baggage here before entering. Customers wearing coats and hats, please remove them.

"Miss Fran, what is this?"

"We might as well go with the flow. Let's follow the unique rules of this restaurant."

She was already removing her cloak as she spoke.

"...Sigh..."

If that's the rule, I guess I'll follow it. Though I have absolutely no idea why on earth they would set up all these doors like this...

After we had both removed our cloaks and hats, Miss Fran and I opened the door in front of us.

But...

Our deepest apologies, but our restaurant is very sensitive to smell. Before opening the next door, please apply a spritz of perfume.

Apparently, the proprietor of this restaurant was a very fussy individual, despite the shabby appearance of the place.

In front of the door was a small stand, with a bottle of perfume sitting on it bearing a label that read HELP YOURSELF.

"Miss Fran, what is this?"

"Just go with the flow..."

"...Again?"

With an experienced hand, Miss Fran sprayed herself with the perfume. A sweet, fruity aroma filled the air. I impatiently wondered when on earth we might be getting some food. In contrast, Miss Fran seemed incredibly calm. It wasn't at all clear who had invited whom for a meal.

I had to ask.

"Miss Fran, I'd like to ask you something before we go any further."

"Yes?"

"This isn't one of those weird theme restaurants, where we're going to end up getting cooked by giants or something, is it?"

"Oh-hoh-hoh!"

"Would you mind answering my question instead of laughing at me?"

I narrowed my eyes intently, and Miss Fran smiled.

"You'll get your answer after we open the next door...," she said as she pushed the door open.

Cautiously, I followed my teacher through.

We had been made to remove our shoes and our cloaks and relinquish our baggage. On top of that, we'd had to spray ourselves with some strange-smelling perfume. I wondered what on earth we might be compelled to order after we got inside.

To be perfectly honest—and I hate admitting this—but as reluctant as I was to proceed, I was getting a little bit curious about this strange restaurant.

"……"

But the place had seemingly already outwitted me.

As we opened this door, I half expected to find another small room waiting for us. But instead, there was a completely ordinary dining room.

In short, we had finally arrived inside the restaurant.

"Sorry for the delay, Elaina." Miss Fran chuckled pleasantly. "This is The Giants' Kitchen."

I was surprised by how quiet the interior was. There was no greeting from any staff or anything. It was utterly still.

Actually...

"Um, I don't see the owner..."

Inside the cramped restaurant was a single table with a set of chairs around it, and a kitchen in the back. That was it. It looked less like a restaurant and more like a typical kitchen you'd find in a private home.

The proprietor must have expected us. They had left cookies for the two of us sitting on the table.

"Miss Fran, what is this?"

I stared at the cookies as I took a seat. They were displayed neatly on a plate, and they were all long, thin rectangles, a strange shape for cookies.

"That's our appetizer," she answered without hesitation as she sat down across from me.

"Uh-huh…"

I don't really understand what's going on, but if nothing else, this does not, in fact, appear to be a restaurant where giants prepare dishes using humans as ingredients.

"By the way, I don't see any sign of these giants," I said as I picked up a cookie and snapped it in half.

"……"

But Miss Fran didn't give me any kind of answer; she just covered her mouth with one hand and started shaking with silent laughter.

"…What's wrong?"

"…Oh, nothing…"

"…Sigh…"

As I munched on my cookie, I tilted my head questioningly at my teacher, who was behaving quite strangely.

"So where are the giants?" I inquired again.

After catching her breath, Miss Fran replied, "The giants are already here."

●

Effective today, I will be assuming responsibility as record keeper, in place of Liscia, who succumbed to insanity after the battle a few days ago.

The job of the record keeper is not easy. I must always be on the front lines, in order to record our battles against the giants. By no means can I condemn Liscia for losing heart. From the moment one assumes this post, a record keeper is constantly fighting to keep hold of their mind.

So it's not like I can complain.

Besides, I'm sure that the captain has it even worse than a new recruit like me. Our leader has had to constantly throw the troops under her command into battle against the giants ever since the day we took up this position.

"Are you getting used to your job as record keeper, Acre?"

The captain looked at me as she surveyed the fortress that was being repaired after the previous battle with the giants. Her features were hearty and healthy, and she was a strong, dignified woman.

"Captain…"

"What is it?"

"I just assumed the position of record keeper today, so I'm not used to this crap at all."

"You've got a mouth on you, Acre."

"Always have, ma'am. Get used to it."

"It'll take me a while to get used to it…"

"Same goes for my job as record keeper, ma'am."

There's nothing to do but get over it. Hopefully I'll have time to get used to the job.

"Captain! There's trouble!" one of the sentries called, looking suddenly grim.

I had a bad feeling.

"…What is it?"

The captain's face changed, too. The air suddenly became tense.

After catching her breath for a moment, the sentry announced, "Giants have invaded our fortress!"

It looked like I wasn't going to get any time to get used to my new job after all, or have the chance to get to know the captain better.

"What did you say...?! Impossible, it's too soon...! It hasn't even been a week since we withstood the last attack!"

A giant had invaded our fortress just a few days earlier. There were no formal records, since Liscia had lost her wits in the middle of the battle, but I had heard that the casualties were considerable.

And now our enemy had appeared again. We hadn't even had a chance to recover from the previous attack.

We were as shocked as you would expect.

But the captain was calm. "Describe the enemy. We'll deal with them immediately. What are we up against?"

"It's"—the lookout faltered as she answered—"the same giant as before..."

"...What was that?"

"The black-haired giant that attacked us last time has come back to attack again...!"

"I see...back for revenge?"

"That's not all!" The lookout raised his voice again.

Then she reported the dreadful truth to the captain, whose expression had stiffened slightly.

"She brought a friend...!"

"What...?"

It wasn't that she had failed to hear the guard's words. She couldn't believe it.

"This time the giant has brought a companion with her...! There is another female giant by her side, this one with gray hair!"

Two giants had shown up at once. As far as I could remember, this was the first time that had ever happened. What's more, one of them was known to us as the "black devil," the horrible creature who had broken the previous record keeper's sanity.

"I see... It seems that devil means to slaughter us in earnest..."

The captain stubbornly feigned composure. But I dutifully recorded the fact that a single bead of sweat rolled down her cheek.

* * *

Our fortress has multiple layers of traps set up as anti-giant measures. These are our unique means of combat, devised over a long history of battling giants.

Our tactics are always evolving.

Welcome to The Giants' Kitchen. You must be tired. Please remove your footwear.

The first trap is set up right after they open the first door, to get them to take their footwear off. The giants are deceived by our polite wording and heedlessly remove their shoes.

Sure enough, the two giants had taken off their shoes.

"Heh-heh-heh…these devils never learn. They obediently removed their shoes this time as well…!"

The captain's face relaxed once she had verified from a distance that the devils had both removed their shoes. The first tactic was a success.

Your clothing may get dirty during your stay. Please leave any baggage here before entering. Customers wearing coats and hats may remove those as well.

The most formidable thing about facing down a giant is the thickness of the clothing they cover themselves with. We don't know for sure just what technology is employed to make such garments, but there can be no doubt about the fact that they get in our way. Therefore, we trick the giants into removing their outer garments before entering our fortress.

The stupid black-haired giant had fallen for that trick once again, and her companion with the ash-colored hair had imitated her. Despite their size, giants are significantly inferior to us in terms of intellect.

Our deepest apologies, but our restaurant is very scent-conscious. Before opening the next door, please apply a spritz of perfume.

That was writing on the last door they'd passed through, and of course, this, too, was a piece of strategy. The giants have very keen noses. They are able to sense our presence by scent alone, so the perfume disguises our smell and keeps them from detecting us.

"Our total victory is assured in this battle, isn't that right, Captain?"

All I felt was absolute admiration for the captain's brilliant planning. As long as we had our strategies in place, which had performed perfectly to date, we could surely seize victory in the coming conflict. I was certain of it.

"...Don't get careless, Acre."

But the captain wore a gloomy expression.

"I haven't forgotten the losses of the previous battle."

She was talking about that time...

"H-hey...Captain...! Captain..."

The former record keeper, Liscia, had approached the captain on the battlefield. "Gimme some leaves...leaves, now!" she said, clinging to the captain. "If I don't have 'em, I'm done forrr...!" She had seemed almost mad.

After that last battle, Liscia had changed. All she did was demand leaves, day after day. She was broken, reduced to nothing more than a leaf junkie.

Such was the fate of the record keeper who had been so devoted to her duties. I had felt a chill run up my spine.

"Let go of me!" The captain had torn Liscia off her. "...Listen up, Acre. Unexpected circumstances always arise during battle. Just don't let your guard down."

It had seemed like she was issuing an unspoken threat that "this is what will happen to you if you're not careful."

But were we really going to have any problems this time? As far as I could see, the two giants who had entered our fortress were being manipulated by the captain's scheme.

Actually, they didn't suspect a thing, even now that they were sitting inside.

Without knowing that it was the signal for us to commence a battle against them, the giants had taken their seats.

"All hands, advance!"

At the captain's signal, the soldiers picked up their weapons and charged. It was going to be a brief yet decisive battle, an all-out assault. This, too, was part of the captain's strategy.

We simply didn't have the stamina for a drawn-out campaign.

Therefore, we needed to engage the giants immediately and quickly drive them away.

However…

"Captain! Big problem! We have no weapons!"

"What did you say?!"

There was nothing in the warehouse where the weapons should have been stored. It was completely empty.

"Oh no, Captain! For some reason, we left our weapons on the giants' table!"

"What did you say?!"

Why didn't anyone notice until now?

Our weapons had been left on the tabletop.

"Who was the idiot who left them in a place like that!?" The captain raised her voice in irritation.

"Eh-heh-heh…" Liscia laughed.

"Why yooooooouuuuuu!" The captain grabbed her by the collar.

"Wait…Captain, calm down, please…!"

She seemed worked up enough to throw a punch at any moment. I rushed over to try to grab the captain from behind and stop her, but she pummeled Liscia brutally with her small fists. "Do you have any idea how foolish a mistake that was?! Damn you!"

"Eh-heh, eh-heh-heh…"

Liscia almost seemed to enjoy the beating. I don't think it was a side effect of the leaves either… She'd always seemed weird that way.

"Captain, terrible news!"

"What is it this time?!" the captain shouted. Any semblance of calmness and composure was nowhere to be seen.

"Look at that!"

One of the soldiers pointed. There was one of the enemies we were supposed to be confronting—one of the giants.

There she was, one of those disgusting giants, chomping away on one of the weapons that we had held so dear.

"What…the…?"

She was eating our weapons.

A scene that none of us could have imagined, spread out right there before our eyes.

There was nothing to do but tremble with fear.

Unexpected circumstances always arise during battles, after all.

○

"Um, by any chance, are *we* the giants?"

Ever since we had come to this restaurant, I hadn't caught so much as a glimpse of any staff, so I'd been discreetly looking around the place, and had noticed some…strange details.

"Seems like you've figured it out."

"…Yeah, I guess."

Straining my eyes to take a close look toward the kitchen, I saw a girl dressed in armor, and another girl beside her wearing glasses, scribbling desperately. With them were many others, including a girl who was constantly cackling with laughter.

The surprising thing was their size.

Unless it was some trick of the eye, they were each small enough to fit in the palm of my hand. They looked human, but it was hard to see them as regular people because of how small they were.

"This place, which they named 'The Giants' Kitchen,' is a trap that they built to take down humans like us."

"Why do they think we're their enemies…?"

"Actually, I came here about a week ago and got them to tell me a little bit about it."

"Oh?"

"According to what they told me, it pretty much boils down to the fact that we're too big, and they don't like it."

"That's a really superficial reason to hate someone…"

"True, but they make really tasty food, so it's pretty convenient to have them here, in the middle of an otherwise empty wilderness."

"Speaking of food…I can't imagine anything served by people that small will be especially satisfying…" *Actually, the first issue is…* "They haven't even emerged from the kitchen yet, have they?"

"There's no need to worry." Miss Fran pointed to my pocket and said, "Earlier, we collected lots of flowers and grasses and acorns, right?"

"If my memory serves me, you just crammed them into my pockets, but…"

"Try pulling a little bit of that stuff out."

Sure, no problem, but…

"Why? Did they tell you that they like common weeds and flowers?"

As I puzzled this over, I went ahead and pulled out a bit of plant matter.

Immediately after I did—

"Ahh! Leaves! I love leaves!"

A girl about the size of my palm suddenly appeared on the table and crouched over the grass, laughing maniacally.

"……"

I was silent.

"These girls really like common weeds and flowers, you see."

"……"

Is this little tribe of people an endangered species or something?

●

"Captain! Terrible news! Liscia has been captured by the enemy!"

"Yes, I know!"

It was plain to see.

Even though only a few minutes had gone by since the beginning of the battle against the giants, the fighting had already claimed one victim. Looming over Liscia, who had run out onto the table, the giant with ash-colored hair spoke.

"Huh...looking at them close up, they're really cute, aren't they...?"

As the giant's repulsive voice boomed, she poked at Liscia with her fingertip.

"Oww!" Liscia toppled over. Then the giant's finger casually pushed on her stomach several times.

"Heh-heh-heh..." The giant laughed.

Disgusting. The ashen-haired giant had only just captured Liscia and was already showing no intention of treating her as human.

"That monster...! She's torturing Liscia!" The captain's expression was steeped with hatred.

But there was nothing that we could do. We were powerless before the giants.

"Ah...! St-stop it...! Ah-ha...!"

But the giant didn't stop.

Instead, the ashen-haired giant put on a pleasant smile as she stared down at the struggling Liscia.

"You want leaves? Which leaves? These? Or these over here?"

An unbelievably dreadful scene was playing out before our very eyes. After tickling Liscia's belly for a little while, the giant feigned bringing leaves close to Liscia's face, then started tickling her again.

"Stop...! Ah, I love leaves... Stop it... Ahhh!"

This is torture.

Receiving pain and pleasure at the same time, Liscia was gradually losing her mind.

"That must be irresistible for a masochist."

"Should we be doing something, or...?"

On the other hand, Liscia has always been kind of strange.

Meanwhile, on the tabletop, the ashen-haired giant seemed to be having fun toying with Liscia.

"Heh-heh-heh-heh-heh..." She cackled.

"......"

The giant didn't seem to have noticed the icy gaze coming at her from across the table.

Then the ashen-haired giant who had been toying with Liscia for a while suddenly stopped moving her hands.

"Ah-ha—huh?" Liscia was taken aback when the tickling and the leaves were abruptly withdrawn. She sat up and stared at the giant with a pleading expression.

"You want more?" The ashen-haired giant was in high spirits now. "If you want more…could I get you to tell me about your companions? They're over there, right? How many are hiding?"

It was a foolish question.

"Tch…it's no use." Beside me, the captain let slip a smile. "The bonds of military service are unbreakable. There is no way that Liscia will ever give up her comrades. She may be off her rocker, but she'd never stoop so low as to sell the rest of us out—"

"There are thirteen."

She did, in fact, stoop so low.

"Any weapons?"

"You ate all of them a minute ago."

"Oh-hoh. So that means that all of your companions are unarmed— Wait, huh? I *ate* them? What do you mean, I ate them…?"

Then Liscia easily spilled all the information she had to the enemy—everything, starting with the captain's strategy. She didn't hesitate to reveal it all. The girl on the table was now the lowest of worthless wretches, calmly selling out her comrades for leaves.

"I see; it's all clear now."

After making Liscia tell all, the ashen-haired giant nodded heartlessly. "By the way, I came here today to have a meal, you know."

Her eyes seized on us.

Those eyes, a lapis blue color that threatened to suck me right in, abruptly narrowed, and a smile appeared on the giant's face.

And then she said, "I'm guessing there's food over there in the kitchen, right?"

Food...?

"She wants to eat...! She's going to gobble us up, every one of us...!"

I'm sure I don't need to tell you that everyone in the kitchen shuddered with fear.

○

"Elaina. If you go into the kitchen, we'll never get any food."

Just when I thought that we were finally going to get to eat, after being teased for so long, Miss Fran spoke up with a sigh.

Huh?

"Aren't we going to plunder food from these tiny girls?" I asked.

"Absolutely not, they would just run away..."

For some reason, Miss Fran had really drawn back. I wondered what on earth I had done to warrant that reaction.

It seemed like Miss Fran was a repeat customer here at The Giants' Kitchen. Her tone suggested that she knew everything about the place, though I had my doubts.

"There's no need to make any deliberate moves. Now that you've captured one of their friends, it won't be long."

"Won't be long for what?"

"For the food to come out."

Immediately after she'd said that, I heard a noise from the kitchen. Something fell down with a crash.

Hey now, what on earth is going on over there? I tilted my head curiously, and I could just barely make out something small squirming over toward us from the kitchen.

"......"

I soon understood what I was seeing.

Thirteen tiny girls, each the size of the palm of my hand, had formed a little phalanx and were advancing in our direction. In their hands, they were each gripping some sort of cylindrical object.

"Miss Fran, what is this?"

"It looks like they've brought us something to eat."

"Huh...?"

I tilted my head the other way.

Each of the tiny girls was carrying a sweet treat—not exactly what I'd expected for a meal.

The blond girl leading the charge was carrying a long, round cookie. Beside her was a girl in glasses, who was still desperately writing, balancing a macaron on her head.

Behind them, the girls grouped into columns had also armed themselves with various sweets. They appeared wielding cookies, chocolates, and similar bite-sized treats.

"...Um, what is going on here?"

My face contorted in confusion, but Miss Fran nodded, "The truth is, their species excels at making sweets."

"Uh-huh..."

"But apparently, they don't eat the sweets they make."

"What does that mean?"

"To them, the sweets are used as building materials, or to make weapons, even. They're more like a resource than food."

It sounded like their species saw things very differently. To us, the things they made were nothing more than tasty treats.

"......"

So when it comes down to it...

"In other words, they've armed themselves and are coming to do battle with us?"

"Well, to put it bluntly, that's what it amounts to."

"......"

By the way, just a moment ago, Miss Fran said something about "the food arriving," but...

"Huh, you mean we're going to eat their weapons?"

"Indeed."

Miss Fran nodded easily, as if this were completely normal.

"...What will happen when we eat them?"

"Their resources will be depleted, of course."

"……"

"Well, now seems as good a time as any. Shall we begin our teatime?"

Miss Fran wore a carefree smile as a voice echoed from the direction of the kitchen.

"Chaaaaaarge!"

I wonder if there has ever been such a brutal teatime before…

●

"Don't worry, everyone. Our enemy is enormous, and we have no weapons. But if we don't have any weapons, we can just make more."

Following Liscia's utter betrayal, the captain ran over to the empty warehouse.

"Let's break down this warehouse to make weapons."

As she spoke, the captain snapped off a piece of the warehouse wall. The wall was brittle and fairly easy to break. A faintly sweet scent filled the air, and the captain turned back toward us, her soldiers, who seemed to be facing a hopeless battle.

"There are times when we must fight." Our captain looked courageous and strong, as always. "That time is now! All hands, tear this warehouse apart and prepare to charge!"

The captain was always able to find a way out of trouble, no matter how desperate the situation. *As long she's with us, we have no reason to worry.* I'm certain that's what everyone was thinking. We all exchanged looks, and without saying a word, we each picked up our own weapons.

"As the record keeper, I'm going to ask you to come with us to the battlefield, but I won't make you carry a weapon. Acre, it is your duty to leave behind a record of this battle for posterity. Put this on."

The captain placed an unfamiliar round yellow object on my head.

"…Um, Captain, what's this?"

"It's material that was used to make the warehouse roof. It's brittle, but it should protect your head, at least."

"Captain..."

Wait, we're fighting giants. Protecting my head isn't going to do anything...

"Don't worry. I'm going to protect you, I swear. Protecting my comrades is what I do!"

"Captain..."

"Acre, you just carry out your duties. Make a record of this battle and return with your life."

"Captain..."

"Come on, you don't need to be that nervous. Once the battle is over, let's go for a drink, okay?"

"Captain..."

Just now, I thought I smelled the stench of death wafting through the air... It must have been my imagination.

"All right, let's go, everyone!"

Ignoring my concerns, the captain stood at the front of the formation and looked up at the giants. *There are times when we must fight. Even when we know we will lose.*

And then...

The captain sucked in a determined breath, and—

"Chaaaaaarge!"

Our fateful battle began.

"Oh, Elaina, a moment ago you took a leaf out of your pocket. You should still have all sorts of things stashed away in there, right?" Looking down at us, the black-haired giant said, "How about pulling some of those things out?"

"Suppose I could."

Grinning like the devil she was, the ashen-haired giant pulled her hand out of her pocket and opened it on top of one of the huge white platters.

"......!"

It was at this moment that we finally realized the gravity of our own error.

Liscia's capture, this attack of ours—everything was part of the scheme devised by the giants.

We were nothing more than pawns in their enormous hands.

"These are what you want, right...?"

On top of the white platter, she'd scattered leaves, flowers, and acorns.

It was unbelievable.

The giants had come prepared with a strategy to get us to lay down our weapons. They were obviously cunning opponents who understood their enemy.

But there was no way we would be led astray.

Because we had to emerge victorious against them.

There's no way that there is anyone here on this battlefield right now who is enough of a fool to fall into such an obvious trap—

"Leave this area to me! The rest of you, go on aheeead!"

For some reason, the captain had thrown herself down atop the white platter. She had even tossed her weapon aside nearby. She no longer had even the tiniest glimmer of fighting spirit in her.

"Captain..."

What the hell is she doing?

"Don't worry...I'll definitely catch up with you later...!"

"No, um, Captain..."

The immediate capture of their leader sent the remaining troops into disarray. They milled to and fro like a bunch of wild beasts.

They lost all fighting spirit at the sight of their captain's pitiful showing.

"It can't be...! The captain is...!" One girl sank into despair and threw down her weapon.

"Wait for me, Captain! I'm coming to save—gyaaah!" One girl tried to jump onto the white platter, slipped carelessly, and fell down.

"Heh-heh...it's all over now..." One girl gave up entirely and started to make herself at home on the platter.

"Why, you! I was the first one to find this flower!"

"Shut up! What does that have to do with anything?! Hand it over now!"

There were even girls fighting with their comrades over flowers, of all things.

One after another, my compatriots abandoned their weapons.

"So, you see, just like when I came here last week, they've given us a lot of sweets. Apparently, they have a weakness for leaves, flowers, and acorns, and all you have to do is give them some to get a bunch of sweets in return."

"...To me, it looks more like a revolt than anything else, though..."

The two giants picked up the weapons that my comrades had dropped and, without taking any notice of our suffering, tossed our weapons, one after another, into their gaping maws.

From the way they were acting, they didn't even seem to consider us a threat.

Either that, or they were showing off their absolute dominance. No matter how we might struggle, we had no way to retaliate against the giants.

"Oh? There's only one of them left."

Suddenly, the black-haired giant's gaze landed on me. Looking across the table, only I, the record keeper, was still outside the borders of the white platter. Now that everyone else was imprisoned on the platter, I was the sole survivor.

"You're right."

The ashen-haired giant nodded and peered down at me with her lapis-colored eyes.

"...Ah!" She clapped her hands and fished around in her pocket.

She was probably going to try to bait me with grass, or flowers, or acorns, or another one of our favorites.

But there's no way that I can die! I must live on for the sake of my fallen comrades—

"I think you'll probably like this."

What she handed me then was a mysterious disk. It was round, and glossy, and sparkled like gold. It was profoundly heavy.

I've heard rumors about these.

In the world of the giants, those golden, sparkly disks were known as "money" and could apparently be exchanged for goods or services. No one in our world had ever laid eyes on one before, but there were persistent rumors that anyone who touched one would be able to, at the very least, live the rest of her life in leisure.

"Ah…so shiny…"

Needless to say, I fell right into the enemy's hands. I abandoned the duties that the captain had given me, and just like my fallen comrades, I surrendered.

Looking down at me as I rubbed my cheek lovingly against the shiny gold, the black-haired giant opened her eyes wide. "You really knew what she would like, didn't you?"

In response, the ashen-haired giant popped the armor that I was wearing on my head into her mouth and said, "Oh, I just sort of saw that same look in her eye."

"Ah, you mean she's greedy like you?"

"How rude. I prefer to think I'm 'devoted to my desires.'"

And so our battle came to an end.

It goes without saying that we suffered a crushing defeat. At least that's what I thought.

But from the center of the white platter, our captain announced with satisfaction, "Phew…this battle was an absolute victory for our side…"

○

Once we'd left The Giants' Kitchen, Miss Fran finally told me the story of her visit to the restaurant the previous week.

Apparently, she had come across the place on her way to her hometown.

"This is embarrassing, but I've got a terrible sense of direction, and also, I haven't been home once since I set out on my own travels…so I got completely lost. I was traveling along, asking directions from every merchant and traveler I passed, but…"

Um, I'm actually trying to go to a country called Bielawald, but— huh? No such country exists anymore? All right, well, the former site will be fine, so could you tell me where it is? Huh? In the forest? I'm sorry, there's nothing but forest around here, so specifically, what part of the forest is it in? Ah, that way? …I see…

Excuse me, but the merchant I asked earlier said that Bielawald was in this part of the forest, so…huh? There's no such country? No, I know it exists. The ruins will be fine; can you tell me where they are? Huh? In the forest over there? Wait, but it's forest as far as I can see—

And so on.

One way or another, Miss Fran had apparently continued her journey, wandering from place to place.

And in the middle of all of that, she had discovered this cottage.

When she'd first come across the place, the sign declaring it to be THE GIANTS' KITCHEN hadn't yet been on display. She told me that it had been nothing but an ordinary little house.

"At first, I was in shock. When I snuck into the cottage to get some rest, I never expected to find a race of tiny women living inside."

According to Miss Fran, as one would expect, the tiny women had seemed to fear humans of our size. They had surprised her with a sudden attack.

"Though, of course, their attacks don't present any threat to us humans, so I also hardly paid them any mind."

For example, the so-called artillery that had been launched at her were just sugar candies, and the things that the little ladies had been holding up as shields had been ordinary cookies. She had squared off against the pastry-clad women, but from Miss Fran's perspective, they had just looked like strange, little creatures who were showering her with treats. We think that, from their perspective, it must have gone down in history as a gruesome, protracted battle.

After being showered with sweets for a while, Miss Fran must have started feeling a little pang of conscience about the one-sided exchange. She had asked one of the women about it.

"Um, is there anything you would like in return?" she'd asked.

One of them—the one named Liscia—had answered with hatred in her eyes.

"Something we want? Of course not, how could there be?! Get out of here at once!"

My, my, why on earth would she be so bitter toward me?

Miss Fran had wondered what the reason might be.

At that point, she'd had an idea.

"I feel bad just taking, without offering anything in return… I wonder if I have anything I can give you…?"

But because Miss Fran was always such a carefree person, when she searched her pockets, the only things she had found were a few leaves she'd happened to shove in there during her travels, and some flowers she'd picked because she'd thought they were pretty, and a handful of acorns that she'd collected for some reason or other. It was all just rubbish.

Oh no! They won't be happy with this stuff. Far from it! It'll probably be a nuisance.

That's what she had thought anyway.

"Aaah! I love these! This smell…! I love it!"

But then something unexpected had happened. The tiny woman had grabbed the leaves Miss Fran had produced from her pocket and started breathing heavily.

The strange developments kept on happening.

One after another, Liscia's companions, who had been stealthily watching everything from nearby, had appeared, and they had all started fighting over the rubbish that Miss Fran had produced, saying things like, "What is this?" "Oh, flowers!" "I love acorns…" "Hey, hey, this is out of this world…!"

Apparently, they had hardly ever seen the flowers and leaves that litter the outside world. The cottage was their whole world.

One after another, the tiny women had dropped their weapons, and Miss Fran had eaten her fill of them (the sweets, that is).

After the soldiers had all given up, the one whom everyone called "Captain" had stood before Miss Fran and raised a white flag as she announced, "Gah...we're no match for you... Do as you will, Giant. Boil us, roast us, eat us alive...!"

Wait, wait—

"No, thank you."

I've already gotten all the sweets I want—Miss Fran had shaken her head.

There had been something more important weighing on her mind.

"By the way, why do you all think I am your enemy?"

"Is it not natural to try and drive away intruders?!" The captain had been extremely angry. In a full-blown rage, even. "Plus, you're a dirty cheater! Using our favorite foods to bribe your way to victory—does your cowardice know no bounds?!"

"Oh, favorite foods? Do you mean these?" Miss Fran had casually waved a leaf toward the captain's face.

"Ah...s-stop it! I won't be tempted!" The captain had swatted the leaf away.

Then the captain had told Miss Fran about their circumstances.

The tiny women loved acorns and leaves, but there were many dangers in the outside world, so they had no other option but to live in this cottage, she had explained.

Really, they would have liked to go out into the world and eat leaves and acorns to their hearts' content, but even small animals were like giant beasts to them, so they didn't think it would go too well if they tried.

Only inside the cottage were they truly safe.

Surely they couldn't permit enormous humans to come stomping into their safe house with their muddy shoes. So they always tried to drive them out.

Of course, the massive difference in size meant that they had never yet been victorious, but...

"Gah...this is the one and only place where we can feel safe, but... you giants keep breaking in...!"

"......"

At that point, Miss Fran had suddenly had an idea.

Ultimately, the tiny women wanted leaves and acorns, and they were equipped to provide sweets in exchange for them.

Maybe, if they were careful about how they did things, they might be able to make an arrangement that would benefit both parties.

"Um, I've got a suggestion for you. Would you be so kind as to lend me your ear?"

And then Miss Fran made a suggestion to Liscia and the captain.

●

After the two giants had left together, the captain summoned me, the record keeper, and told me a story. She told me about the problems with our territory, and about what had happened about a week earlier when the black-haired giant had appeared at our door.

"That giant made a suggestion to me. She said, 'We giants want to eat your weapons and building materials. If you let us have them, in return, we'll bring you leaves, and acorns, and flowers.'"

According to the captain, the things that we valued so highly were easy for the giants to acquire, while our weapons and raw materials were apparently their favorite foods. As such, the giant proposed we trade.

"So you accepted her proposal?"

"......" The captain nodded silently. "Since we can make things like weapons and construction materials easily, I figured everyone would be happy to get things from the outside world."

There could be nothing more desirable than a peaceful, mutually beneficial solution. For the sake of the dignity of our race, the captain had accepted the giant's idea.

"Heh-heh-heh...but who would have thought there would be such an easy way to get our hands on leaves... Those giants may have formidable bodies, but their heads are empty...!"

She had accepted the giant's proposal for our sake...or so I'd like to think.

It seemed to me that we had ostensibly suffered a loss in this most recent battle, but apparently, in truth, neither we nor the giants had suffered any damages.

It had been a total farce.

"But, Captain, if both we and they were going to each bring the thing the other wanted, and simply trade, then there was no need to go to the trouble of staging a whole battle, was there?"

Was there any need for us to go through the motions of driving the giants away, like we did when we didn't know anything about them? It sounds like we could have concluded the whole interaction by appearing before them, presenting them with some building materials, and grabbing what we wanted in return.

Wasn't rallying the troops for a glorious last stand actually kind of pointless?

But the captain just nodded, then said, "It was the black-haired giant's suggestion that we wage battle. She asked me to be sure to launch an attack just like we did last time."

"...Why?"

"Apparently it was more interesting that way."

"I really don't understand how those giants think."

"Me either."

○

"...Huh, so in other words, if we give them leaves and stuff in exchange for sweets, those little ladies will be satisfied with the exchange?" I asked. "Is that what you're saying?"

"Well, to make a long story short, yes." Miss Fran nodded.

We'd left The Giants' Kitchen behind, continuing to our next destination. As we traveled, we chatted about what had happened.

"But then why did they try to attack us? If we were going to exchange sweets for leaves, shouldn't that have been the end of it?"

"Who knows? I wonder why?"

My teacher looked out into the distance, wearing a devious smile. Frankly speaking, the fact that she basically averted her eyes from me made it somewhat obvious that she was hiding something, but I decided to hold my tongue.

When it came down to it, the real reason that Miss Fran had guided us to the little women's cottage was so that she could see if they would follow her instructions. The rest was just a pretext.

She had been awfully pushy about leading me there, but now I saw that she had apparently been using me as a test subject.

"Was it fun?" Miss Fran asked.

I nodded halfheartedly. "Sort of."

"Hmm, I see."

Miss Fran nodded, seeming satisfied, and then pulled a piece of paper from her breast pocket and started writing something very misleading: *Received a rave review from the world-traveling Ashen Witch!*

What's this?

"Wait a minute, what are you doing?"

I grasped Miss Fran's hand.

She was holding a pamphlet with phrases on it like, *The dominion of a profoundly mysterious race of tiny people,* and *Eat your fill of their handmade sweets at The Giants' Kitchen,* and *Plan your visit after collecting leaves,* along with a neatly drawn map to The Giants' Kitchen.

"...What is this?" I scowled.

Miss Fran cocked her head, puzzled. "What is it...? It's business."

Huh? Business?

"...Don't tell me you're thinking of making a profit off them?"

"No, no, I was just going to spread the word about a rare species, with the best of intentions."

"......"

Looking at the pamphlet, I could see that she had written instructions on the edge: *Gladly accepting a finder's fee, in the amount you deem appropriate.*

It seemed particularly devious, keeping the exact sum vague. If she felt like it, she would be able to overcharge people by pressuring them after the fact.

My, my.

"How greedy you are."

I gazed wearily at my teacher.

In her usual nonchalant way, she smiled and replied, "How rude. I'm simply 'devoted to my desires.'"

Dear me, I wonder where Miss Fran learned such things...?

"Miss Fran, you are my teacher, so it makes things difficult for me when you refuse to behave with anything approaching decency or maturity."

I made a point of puffing out my cheeks, but Miss Fran just smiled as she always did.

"Unfortunately, I may be your teacher, but I am also myself."

Oh my, well then...

"You're a real lowlife of a teacher, you know that?"

"Oh, I agree."

CHAPTER 2

A Country Girl, a History Addict, and a Potion Dosing

I've heard it was around seven or eight years ago, or thereabouts, when news of the mysterious place known as The Giants' Kitchen began to spread among travelers.

Pamphlets claiming that a certain traveling witch—the Ashen Witch, who had traveled the world over—had given it a rave review started circulating among tourists. Eventually, for a certain segment of the population, these pamphlets became quite valuable.

Even now, the pamphlets seem to have retained their value, considering that even my own traveling companion was clutching one to her chest like a precious object as she said, "This pamphlet, I can't believe it... I finally got my hands on one at an auction... I'm in love..."

"By the way, this Ashen Witch...could that be our teacher, by any chance?"

I pointed to the bottom of the pamphlet that my companion was holding. There was a silhouette printed there alongside the Ashen Witch's endorsement. It was a figure I had seen before.

"I have the same feeling." My companion nodded.

And then she looked up at the dilapidated building rising before us.

There was a sign hanging on the front door that read, CLOSED FOR RENOVATIONS, though the state of the place gave off the sense that, far from being closed for renovations, it was closed for good.

"Huh? But the pamphlet says they're open every day of the year, doesn't it...?"

How strange. What on earth could this mean?

"Hmph!" My traveling companion smiled unexpectedly. "It looks like they made arrangements so that no one would enter the restaurant by mistake. But that's fine. I'm sure that this sign is a lie," she said, before tossing the CLOSED FOR RENOVATIONS sign away.

"Should you do that?"

"It's fine. The pamphlet was right after all."

Apparently, my companion placed a great deal of confidence in this pamphlet that she had worked so hard to acquire (all she did was win it at an auction).

"I'm sure they don't want random travelers wandering in here. Nobody is even supposed to know about the existence of this restaurant unless they have the pamphlet… Heh-heh…heh-heh-heh-heh…"

My traveling companion, a girl named Linaria, who had her purple hair tied up in a single ponytail behind her head, placed one hand on the door.

Standing behind her, watching her with very cold eyes, was the chestnut-haired Alte.

"……"

…*By which I mean myself.*

We were currently right in the middle of a history hunt, exploring the history of various countries.

What on earth is a history hunt, you ask?

And what awaited us on the other side of that door?

Before I tell you how Linaria went even crazier after touching a genuine piece of history, I suppose I must tell you how we wound up in a place like this.

Let me wind back the clock to around one week earlier, when all of this began.

Latorita State University has a long vacation period, from late winter until early spring.

Most students visit home during the break, and I'd also made plans to go show my smiling face to my family in the countryside as usual; however, this year I had no choice but to abandon that plan. It had nothing to do with suddenly needing supplemental lessons because I'm not too clever, or with being busy at my part-time job, or anything like that.

There was something else going on.

"I'm going traveling."

Late at night, the day before the start of vacation, my friend Linaria suddenly appeared at my dorm room, waking me from a deep sleep to happily tell me some urgent news.

"I'm using the long vacation to set out on a journey and go on a history hunt. A history hunting trip…heh-heh-heh…"

Linaria was so excited that she didn't seem to care what time it was.

When we'd first met, I'd thought that she was really cool and awesome. But apparently, when it came to history, she became a bit unhinged.

At first, the sudden changes that came over her had perplexed me, but eventually, I got used to them. Now she was suddenly barging into my room at all hours, rambling on about who knows what. But we were friends, so I didn't want to shut her down.

"Ah, come to think of it, you've been saying something like that for a while, haven't you…? Fwaah…" I let out a yawn.

Still dazed, I thought back on the past, almost as if I were slipping into a dream.

I recalled a moment between classes.

Linaria had come to show me a weathered old pamphlet that was obviously suspicious.

"Listen, apparently there's a strange restaurant not far from here called The Giants' Kitchen. The tiny women there view us humans as their enemies and try to attack the patrons. Despite them being tiny, the place is called The Giants' Kitchen. Doesn't that strike you as a contradiction? I think it is. It's awfully mysterious."

And another time, when the two of us were picking at our lunches, she had held a one-sided conversation.

"Apparently there's a certain country where there are plaster busts lining the walls of the historical archives, including one of a goddess. I've heard that the goddess was repaired about seven years ago and the new bust is simply stunning. Don't you think it would be worth visiting?"

Or once, when we were on the way home from school, she had talked with great excitement about something.

"I heard that there is a country where they've been holding broom races for ages. Apparently, many travelers gather there from all over, hoping for their chance to strike it rich by betting on the outcome of the race. Honestly, I don't care too much about the race or the money, but historically speaking, countries that hold such races are quite rare. Wouldn't you like to go see that?"

I remembered one time when the two of us were soaking next to each other in the dorm baths, and she was jabbering on.

"This reminds me, speaking of baths, I heard that in a place fairly far from here, there's an underwater city called the Sunken City. Until recently, it was thought to be a ruin, but actually, the people of the Sunken City had cut off contact with the outside world and continued living in isolation. Don't you think that's incredible?"

She had been carrying on about such things quite often recently, and for my part, I had been giving perfunctory answers like "I see" and "Sounds interesting" during Linaria's impromptu history lectures. She seemed satisfied enough just having someone to talk at and didn't really seem to mind my clipped responses.

"And listen, and—"

Her eyes glistening with excitement, she would speak at length, recounting tales from yesteryear.

That's what had been going on lately.

I knew her well enough that I could guess just how Linaria would make use of the long school break.

"When do you leave…?" I asked with another unsteady yawn.

"What a silly question… Right now, of course!"

Apparently, she was leaving right that minute.

When I rubbed my sleepy eyes and took a better look at her, I could see that Linaria was dressed in her usual school uniform, but she had a huge rucksack on her back.

I see—so she stopped by my room after she got ready.

"Is that so…? All right, I expect souvenirs…*fwah*…"

I let another yawn slip out and started to close the door.

"Huh? Wait. What are you saying?"

I tried to close it, but Linaria stuck her foot in the crack and stopped me. She even put her hand on the door and forced it open again.

"Why aren't you ready?"

Huh?

Ready for what?

"Huh? What do you mean?" At that moment, my drowsiness suddenly fell away.

Huh? Ready? What am I supposed to be ready for?

I couldn't hide my bewilderment. Linaria narrowed her eyes at me in dissatisfaction, then said, "You're coming with me. On my history hunt."

"……"

"……"

Huh?

What is she talking about?

"You promised, didn't you? Have you forgotten?"

Linaria puffed her cheeks out angrily.

Did I promise?

I had just woken up from a deep sleep. My hazy mind went into overdrive, fumbling through past memories just like when we used the time-reversing pocketwatch.

I clearly remembered Linaria talking passionately at me about her history hunt idea whenever she got the chance, but not one instance of getting an invitation.

"I want to go on a history hunt, but…well, it'll be lonely all by myself."

"I see."

Hm?

"So...if it's okay with you, I'm just asking, but...if you want to, how about coming with me?"

"Sounds interesting."

Hmmm?

"......"

"......"

I managed to recall a scene in the baths.

We had been talking and soaking for much too long, and I hadn't really been paying attention when I answered. Now I could see that Linaria had assumed that I was accepting her invitation to join the history hunt. I had even nodded in agreement.

Thinking back, it had seemed like Linaria had been in an unusually good mood ever since then. Now I knew why. She was in high spirits because she'd found a partner for her expedition.

I see, I see.

......

"And I suppose it would be bad if I didn't get ready right now...?"

"That goes without saying."

That was all she said before closing the door.

It was guaranteed that I was going to have a rough time if I wasn't prepared to set out traveling the next time that door opened.

"......"

Dear Father and Mother:

Circumstances dictate that I will not be returning home this year during winter break.

Instead, I will be embarking on some kind of "history hunt," so please expect some nice souvenirs.

○

So that's how Linaria and I ended up setting off on a history hunt together, touring other countries and visiting historic sites.

The first place that we visited on our trip was this cottage that served as the location of The Giants' Kitchen.

Welcome to The Giants' Kitchen. You must be tired. Please remove your footwear.

Apparently, this restaurant had some unique rules in place. I expected to go straight into the restaurant when we passed through the front door, but that wasn't the case. First, we had to take off our shoes.

Apparently, there was already one other customer here before us. A single pair of shoes was placed neatly in the shoe box.

Judging from appearances, they belonged to a woman, but—

Your clothes may get dirty during your stay. Please leave any baggage here before entering. Customers wearing coats and hats, please remove them.

After the shoes, we had to leave our luggage behind. I wondered whether our bags might get stolen if we abandoned them in a place like this, but I figured we had to follow the rules of the restaurant.

Actually, the other customer had left her bags, too, so we followed her lead and set our rucksacks down before opening the next door.

Aren't you thirsty? Before entering our restaurant, please drink this.

That's what we saw when we opened the third door. There was a bottle sitting atop a pedestal with a label attached that read, DRINK ME!

Wow, this Kitchen is really demanding.

I had no real reason to be suspicious, so I picked up the bottle and imbibed some of the contents.

"…Blech!" It had a strange taste. For a clear liquid, it was awfully bitter, and tasted more like medicine than like plain water.

It was absolutely disgusting.

"…Here you go, Linaria."

But it was the restaurant's rules, so we had to drink it.

I expected the history-loving Linaria to drink it down happily and say something like, "Ah! I can taste the history!" I held the bottle out with the mouth of it toward her, but she didn't take it.

"Linaria?"

I tilted my head to the side in confusion.

She wasn't acting like a high-spirited history buff. Instead, she was acting cool and distant.

"That's weird..." Her cold gaze was fixed on the bottle.

"Hm? What's weird?" I was puzzled.

She answered me, "I had heard that you have to pass through three doors to get into The Giants' Kitchen, but the instructions written on this third door are different from the stories I've heard. If I remember correctly, there is supposed to be perfume sitting in front of the third door..."

Oh?

"Then does that mean I might have just drunk perfume...?"

Eww, no wonder it was gross!

"............"

But Linaria slowly shook her head. "Probably that wasn't perfume. The words on the door are also different than in my research."

Huh?

"So then, what on earth..."

What did I just drink?

I took another look at the bottle, and that's when it happened.

"Wah!"

A shock of pain ran through my chest.

My heart was pounding hard, and my breathing grew heavy. I crouched down and dropped the bottle, letting the contents spill out.

As I watched the clear liquid spread out over the floor, I sucked in a deep breath to try to calm my ragged breathing.

But that didn't fix the pain in my chest.

"...! Alte! Are you all right? What's wrong...?"

The sudden throbbing in my chest was so painful that I could only just barely make out the sound of Linaria's panicked voice.

"Ugh...it...hurts..."

I could tell immediately that this pain was eating my body up, worse than any food poisoning. Along with the pain in my chest, I was steadily losing all of my strength.

And then I collapsed.

My body and my clothes got soaked as I fell to the floor.

"Wait, I'll fix you up with a spell!"

Linaria had realized that whatever I had swallowed was not water or perfume, but something more dangerous.

In a panicked rush, she went back to get our bags, and immediately after she'd left...the door to the restaurant opened.

As my vision dimmed, I saw someone appear from the other side of the door, grinning widely.

"Oh-hoh-hoh...welcome to my ideal world!"

Then she picked me right up off the ground and walked back inside the restaurant.

As we moved inside, I noticed something strange.

Somehow, I fit entirely within her cupped hands.

I was snug inside the hands of this girl, who was as big as a giant.

O

When I opened my eyes, I could tell right away that something was amiss.

Apparently, I had been fast asleep in the kitchen, because there was a frying pan and all sorts of cooking utensils lying beside me.

But the strange thing was that all these kitchen utensils were ridiculously huge. For example, the frying pan was big enough that I could easily fit inside it. The knives could have sliced me right in half, and the pots and plates and everything else were all just enormous. The sight made me suspect that I was about to get cooked.

It was literally a giant's kitchen.

"......"

Wait, but maybe...

"Did I...shrink...?"

That was the only answer I could come up with.

I looked up and saw bars. I looked to the front and saw bars. Actually, everywhere I looked, my whole field of vision was covered by bars.

I felt like I was in jail.

Well, it was less like a jail cell and more like a birdcage.

"You're awake."

I sat up and saw someone beside me.

It was a pretty young woman with glasses on.

"Who are you...?"

"I'm Acre. The record keeper."

Record keeper...?

I tilted my head in confusion, and the girl who had called herself Acre said, "So you met with misfortune, too, huh? Ever since that woman came here, this kitchen has changed... This is the punishment pen. When entering our cottage, your body was shrunk down, clothes and all, and she captured you."

She suddenly launched into an explanation.

No...no, no, no.

"Sorry, you're suddenly telling me all these things, and I can't really keep up. Would you mind explaining it from the beginning, step by step?"

"......" Acre wordlessly puffed out her cheeks.

"First of all, where am I?"

"...Don't tell me that you came here without knowing anything about the place?"

"......"

All I could do was nod.

To be honest, Linaria had charged in without inspecting the place or anything, and for my part, it wasn't as if I had been longing to come here out of some passionate interest like Linaria. I didn't really know what kind of establishment this was supposed to be.

Linaria had probably told me all sorts of things about this place before we came here, but since I was in the habit of completely ignoring her when she launched into one of her long talks, I really didn't know anything. I was starting to regret not taking her history lectures more seriously.

"...*Sigh.*" Acre the record keeper let out a sigh. "Well then, read this. I've been acting as the record keeper here at The Giants' Kitchen for a long time, so you ought to understand most everything about this place when you're done."

As she said this, she handed me a book.

She said it contained a record of everything that had happened recently.

I opened the cover.

X month, X day

Compared to how things were several years ago, it seems like our "Giants' Kitchen" has really started thriving. I suppose it's all thanks to those two giants we confronted a little while ago.

From time to time, travelers have been showing up at our doorstep. They gladly present us with the acorns and leaves and flower petals—our favorite foods. In return, we offer them building materials.

This new relationship benefits both parties.

If I had one complaint, it would be that very few humans bring my personal favorite with them.

X month, X day

My favorite is something smooth and shiny called "money" in the outside world. But apparently, it's quite valuable, so despite how readily travelers hand over leaves and stuff, they almost never offer us money. They're so stingy.

Day after day, I perform my duties while rubbing my cheeks against the smooth, shiny piece of gold that the ashen-haired giant gave to me before...eh-heh-heh-heh-heh-heh...so smooth, so shiny, I love it—

* * *

"You don't need to read that part."

I got a kick in the shin when I was in the middle of reading.

"You love money…?"

"Don't look at the parts that have nothing to do with the main story." Acre was huffy with anger. She grabbed the book forcefully from my hands, flipped some pages, and handed it back after opening it to a page with more recent dates.

"That woman came here yesterday."

X month, X day

Today a strange woman came to our restaurant.

She completely ignored our three rules, "remove your shoes," "leave your bags," and "spray yourself with perfume," and marched right in.

When she saw us, she shouted, "Ah! How cute!" and started breathing heavily.

In the course of our work, we have grown used to encountering strange customers. We weren't happy that she hadn't followed the rules, but we started to serve our customer as we always do.

Serve the customer.

In other words, we launched an attack.

The captain roused the troops as usual, and we began preparations for an all-out offensive. If things had proceeded normally, the customer would have observed our oncoming attack and offered us some leaves or something, but on this day, the situation was a little different.

"Oh no, I've been defeated!"

Before we even launched our assault, the woman fell down right on the spot. Then she writhed around in a strangely erotic way. "Go on, do your worst…take my treasure and go…!" From her pockets, she pulled out leaves, acorns, and flower petals, and scattered them all over the floor.

"...What is she doing? We haven't even attacked yet..." The captain also couldn't help feeling uncomfortable about this customer's strange behavior.

"Well, whatever! We win!" But the captain gave in to excitement and declared victory, taking her soldiers along with her to crowd around the leaves.

They were fools.

I greatly prefer the stuff called "money," so I didn't participate in the charge. I just watched from a distance, observing my compatriots' behavior as a record keeper should.

That was how I was able to notice the change coming over them faster than anyone else.

Usually, they would just swarm the offerings and kick up a big fuss, shouting with excitement.

But on this day, everything was different.

"Urk…!"

"What's…happening…?"

"What on earth…?!"

One by one, my compatriots collapsed.

Then, immediately afterward, they abandoned their weapons and staggered back to their feet. Their bodies were limp, and they looked just like they were being hung up by invisible strings.

They stood back up like marionettes.

"Heh-heh…looks like my potion took effect quickly."

Potion.

I'm sure that's what I heard the woman say as she politely reseated herself.

Then she looked down at the soldiers before her.

"From now on, you all work for me. Understand?"

"Yes, ma'am!"

They kneeled. The captain and all the other soldiers and the lookout, they all bowed their heads to the woman in unison.

I immediately understood the situation. All of my comrades were being manipulated by her hand. The leaves and flowers the woman had offered us were having this effect. They had been laced with a potion.

I immediately ascertained her objective.

"Heh-heh-heh…I've already investigated and found that every customer that comes here is rich… They can't get ahold of the pamphlet without winning it at an auction, after all… So if I swindle money off the people who come to this restaurant, I can become very rich indeed…! Ah…what a perfect plan…!"

When I say I "ascertained" it, I mean she just announced it herself.

"Understood, mistress! From now on, we shall extort money from all the invaders!" With tottering steps, my comrades began to clamber up the woman's body. It was impressive how exactly they followed her instructions.

"Ah, wait…! You've got it all wrong! You can stay where you are. Don't move."

"Roger!"

I had no doubt that the effect of the potion didn't extend to me because I hadn't taken the bait that the woman had offered us. However, now that everyone else was under her control except for me, I wasn't safe.

It was clear that if I didn't escape as quickly as possible, that woman would do something to me, too.

"What's this…? One of your little friends is still hiding over there, isn't she…?"

Uh-oh.

As soon as I took a step toward escaping, the woman caught sight of me.

"If you won't listen to what I have to say, I guess I have no choice. Seize her!"

The woman snapped her fingers.

Immediately after that, the others rushed on me, and that pretty much brings us to the present. I was placed here in the punishment pen.

"Heh-heh-heh...with this, the initial preparations are complete." The woman looked down at me now that I was her prisoner and smiled.

That terrible woman's name is Priscilla.

Apparently, she's a young mage.

"You two, there in the punishment pen, how are you doing?"

Immediately after I'd finished reading Acre's long, long record, "that woman" appeared before us.

She had on a soft and fluffy black hat, round with a flat top, and her glossy, golden hair hung down out of the hat in flowing waves. She was dressed in a very distinctive black robe with an elaborate design like a gothic dress.

From the look of her face, I figured she was about the same age as me. But her unusually mature way of talking and her ample figure, which was noticeable even under her thick clothing, made her look less like a lovely young lady and more like an elegant and beautiful adult woman.

I looked up at her from inside the cage.

At the girl dressed in thick, black clothes.

"Isn't that hot?"

Those were the first words that came to mind.

It's early spring now.

You know, spring. And you're dressed for the dead of winter?

When I asked, Priscilla snorted haughtily.

"What a foolish question!"

"Is it a foolish question?"

"Of course it's hot!"

"Oh, it is?"

"But I won't take it off!"

"......"

"Because this is who I am!"

"……"

Priscilla tossed her long hair back. "I've taken custody of your baggage." She hoisted my bag into the air for me to see. "So you're a student? Are you traveling over your long vacation?"

"…That's right."

"Oh-hoh-hoh…but too bad for you! Your journey ends here!"

Priscilla put on a smug look of triumph. She looked mature, but her behavior was certainly appropriate for a girl her age.

"Umm…I'd like you to release me right away…"

"I will not honor that request!" she answered decisively. "If you really must get out, you'll have to steal the key from my minions! By the way, they'll give you a quiz, and if you pass, they'll hand it over!"

"Huh…?"

Priscilla presented me with an unusually specific suggestion for acquiring the key. The little women whom she had already declared to be her "minions" were on standby in front of the cage. She even suggested a difficulty level that seemed way too lenient, by adding, "You can fail the quiz as many times as you need."

"Also, I don't really have any money… Could you please return my bag?"

It makes sense to try to steal from rich customers, but the premise that only rich people would have a pamphlet in the first place is a little bizarre. After all, even a self-supporting student like Linaria managed to save up and win one at an auction.

"I will not honor that request!" As expected, the answer to my proposal was a hard *no*. "If you really must have it back, try and steal it back from me! By the way, I'm going to take a nap now! Are you listening? Don't you dare steal the 'growth potion' that I have in my pocket! If you stole that, you could return your body back to its original size!"

"Why do you keep presenting me with solutions like that?"

It was almost like she was asking me to steal the potion.

"Silence, you! Anyway, I'm going to sleep!"

Priscilla didn't seem the least bit interested in what I had to say. She left the kitchen and went into the dining room, where she huffed as she spread a blanket out on the floor, slapped her pillow several times to puff it up, and stretched herself out for a nap.

Ignoring me as I watched in stunned silence, she did exactly as she had announced and drifted cozily off to sleep.

She looked just like Sleeping Beauty, lying faceup and dozing peacefully.

......

Uh...

"What on earth...?"

At a complete loss, I looked over at Acre, the record keeper. "Can you believe that I have to take a quiz...?!" I balked. "There's no way that I'll be able to answer with the little I know...!"

"You became really dumb all of a sudden, huh?" my caged companion replied. Acre grabbed me by the arm, a little forcefully, and dragged me over to where one minion was standing in front of the cage.

"All right, customer!" the tiny woman outside the cage said. "First of all, you must answer this quiz!"

That's when it happened.

Someone tapped gently on the kitchen window.

When I glanced over, I saw Linaria, looking down at us through a pair of binoculars she held in one hand...from the outside of the dilapidated Giants' Kitchen. The way she peered stealthily through her binoculars at us made her look like she was bird-watching or something. Though her target wasn't a bird; it was just me, in a birdcage.

She stared fixedly at me.

She was holding up a memo pad on which she had written, *You shrank down really small... What happened?*

Of course, right in the middle of all that, the rules of the quiz were being explained to me. The minion who was standing in front of the cage said, "I'm going to give you a quiz now, so please write your answers on this memo pad. If you answer correctly, I'll let you out of the cage. Also, Miss Priscilla said this earlier, but you can retry the quiz no matter how many times you fail." Then she handed me a memo pad and a pen.

......

This is perfect. I can write on here.
I don't really understand what's going on, but for now, I apparently have to take a quiz. I held this up facing the window.

"Ah-ah! I haven't even given you the questions yet! Why are you writing without permission!?" The minion was upset by the interruption.

Quiz...? What do you mean? I don't get it. Linaria cocked her head to the side.

There's a mage named Priscilla here who is trying to take over The Giants' Kitchen, and apparently, she's the reason why this place has gotten so weird. It's her fault I'm like this. I gave a succinct explanation of the situation.

"I told you already! I haven't even asked any questions! Stop writing whatever you want!" The minion was still angry.

I don't really understand, but for now, I just need to take out this Priscilla woman, right?

Please stop saying such unsettling things...

"Unbelievable! You did it again! How many times do I have to say it before you understand?! Wait until I give you the questions! I'm going to get really mad if you do it again!" the minion said, even though she was already fuming.

Behind the minion, Linaria held another piece of paper up for me to read. *Wait there, Alte. I'll come up with something. You take their quiz or whatever and kill some time.*

"All right then, here's your question! Actually, this came up once in Acre's records already. What exactly was the final line that I shouted out in the records she kept? Heh-heh-heh, you got a hard one right off the bat, huh? Well, do you know?"

Paying no attention to what the minion was saying, I held my memo pad up to answer Linaria.

Roger.

"Yes! That's correct!"

The birdcage door opened with a clank.

Huh? What the heck is going on all of a sudden?

I was extremely confused, but I seemed to have unwittingly passed the quiz.

Behind me, Acre seemed impressed. "You're actually quite perceptive…"

The minion also looked pleased. "You're the first one who's ever given the right answer so suddenly, and on your first time taking the quiz, no less…"

"…Huhhh?"

When did I…?

I was totally bewildered, but the other women impatiently began pulling me by the hand before I had fully grasped the situation.

"All right then, proceed to the next stage."

I had been told to wait where I was, so I wanted to remain inside the birdcage until Linaria got to me, but both Acre and the minion insisted that we didn't need the cage anymore, and ultimately, without understand anything that was happening, I was driven out of the cage and then driven out of the kitchen entirely.

At any rate, the only thing I could be sure of was that I had immediately broken my promise to Linaria.

○

"Now that you're out of the cage, all that's left is to steal the potion from Priscilla."

I wanted to go back to the cage, but it seemed like I didn't have that option. With Acre tugging me along by the hand, I wandered around The Giants' Kitchen.

But I knew that Linaria was outside working on some sort of plan, so now that I had left the cage, I couldn't sit around idly doing nothing.

I very much wanted to solve this predicament myself.

To that end, I set off on an adventure, heading toward Priscilla, whom I could see off in the distance, a slumbering giant in this tiny world.

But my journey would not be an easy one.

"Be careful, okay? My comrades are going to come confront you one after another," the minion told me.

Except for Acre, all the tiny women were under Priscilla's control, after all.

It was only to be expected that they would jump in to stop me if I tried to cause any harm to their mistress, Priscilla.

I was first confronted by a single girl, small and cute. She was little enough to fit in a human hand, just like Acre, the first minion, and me.

"Humph…you've done well to make it this far. Now it's time for you to face me in a little game. If you win, I'll let you move on."

Wearing a self-satisfied expression, she challenged me to a game of Othello.

"……"

Othello?

They have Othello in the world of tiny ladies…? Well, I don't mind playing, but…

At any rate, if she's going to bar my path, I suppose I'll have to fight. If I don't, I can't progress.

And if I don't win, of course, I won't be able to make it over to Priscilla. Which means…

"……" I immediately took the corners.

"…Ah." The girl fell into a panic.

"……" I mercilessly colored the top of the board black.

"…Waah." The girl's eyes filled with tears.

I won by an overwhelming margin.

"I could have won even without taking the corners…"

I gave the sobbing girl back to her friends and started walking again.

The next one to block my path was a girl holding a deck of cards.

"Face me in a game of Concentration! I don't mean to brag, but I've never lost before!"

Never lost a round...? Well! She must be a really tough opponent!

...Or so I thought.

"......" I mercilessly collected every pair of cards.

"...Huh?" The girl watched, dumbfounded, as I snatched up the tricks, one after another.

"......" I kept on turning over cards, in spite of the fact that I was already holding the majority in my hand, meaning the match had been decided.

"...Wahhh!" The girl's eyes filled with tears.

Another crushing victory.

I grew up in the country, which meant that we didn't have much to do for fun. I had been playing these sorts of games my whole life.

I had loads of experience.

You could even say I was confident in my abilities.

And so...

After that, the tiny ladies came and challenged me to every conceivable type of game, but I relentlessly defeated every single one of them, made them cry one after another, and worked my way toward Priscilla.

In response to this state of affairs, Acre stared at me. "You heartbreaker...," she muttered, in a way that could have easily been misinterpreted.

Don't look at me that way...

At any rate, after defeating an endless stream of tiny women, there was only one final person standing in my way. She appeared to be a very dour knight.

She didn't tell me her name.

But she was the one whom all the others called "Captain."

"*Tch*...so you made it this far, huh...?"

The little captain, perched atop Priscilla's enormous chest as it rose and fell with her sleeping breaths, looked down at me with a triumphant expression that didn't waver.

"But this is where your steady advance ends! I doubt you will win so easily against me."

Then, with a heave-ho, she produced two pieces of paper and one lottery machine.

After that, she handed one of the slips of paper to me and said, "Here, take this."

"Uh, thanks…" I accepted the paper coldly.

There were rows of numbers on it.

……

It's a BINGO game.

Then the woman started turning the lottery machine with a clatter.

"Ha-ha-ha-ha-ha-ha-ha! Your strengths won't help you in this game! I can triumph through good fortune alone—"

"BINGO."

"Aaaaaaaaaaaahhh!"

Another crushing victory.

After emerging victorious over every one of the tiny women who stood in my way, I climbed up Priscilla's sleeping body and claimed the "growth potion." It was surprisingly anticlimactic, perhaps because humans are fairly defenseless when sleeping. Priscilla didn't show the slightest sign of waking. The whole time I was climbing on top of her, she just kept snoring away.

It was a good thing that she didn't stir in the slightest. I grabbed the potion bottle with the DRINK ME! label on it and immediately pulled off the cap.

She told me…

"If you dash that potion all over your whole body, you'll return to your original size. That's what Priscilla said," said Acre before adding that if I didn't pour it on my clothes, too, only my body would grow larger, which would lead to some unfortunate results.

She seems awfully knowledgeable about Priscilla's business…

"…Um, what is your objective here?"

The whole sequence of events, from when I was placed inside the birdcage up until this very moment, had been indescribably weird. All of Priscilla's minions had given up quite easily after losing their various parlor games.

Wait, actually...

None of this seems necessary to steal money from people. Priscilla could have just tossed me back outside the moment I drank the shrinking potion.

It's like some sort of game...

Whenever one of the girls had challenged me, the mood in the air had been like we were just playing a game together.

"...?" Acre tilted her head at my question. "You're very dull, aren't you...?"

"...Dull?"

What on earth is that supposed to mean?

"Our restaurant is called The Giants' Kitchen," Acre told me.

The reason why Priscilla had made me drink the potion. The reason why Acre had been with me the whole way, almost like a tour guide. The reason why the other girls had challenged me to relatively lazy games.

I put it all together.

"This whole thing has been a demonstration," Acre said.

"......"

"......"

"Demonstration?" I cocked my head.

"Yeah." Acre nodded. "We recently developed a program where customers can experience the world as we see it. We even hired a mage as a part-time employee. That's what's going on."

"......"

"......"

"Part-time?" I gazed at Priscilla, who was murmuring in her sleep.

"Yeah," said Acre. "Priscilla's a part-timer. She's just a regular mage."

"......"

"......"

So that means…what, exactly?

That Priscilla wasn't actually planning to try to steal money from the customers who came to this restaurant? That she was just a regular girl playing the role of an evil mage? And that the majority of the tiny ladies who inhabited The Giants' Kitchen weren't actually being manipulated or anything; they were just playing games with me so that I wouldn't get bored in their tiny world, because it was their job? Is that what this means?

……

Huh? So doesn't that mean that I was never actually a captive at all? So there was no need for me to ask Linaria to save me?

"Oh."

Uh-oh.

These thoughts and more occurred to me, but it was too late.

"You must be Priscilla! Give back my Alte!"

Crash!

Linaria made a heroic entrance by smashing through the window, landing right on Priscilla's sleeping face.

……

Umm…

●

"An 'Incredible Shrinking Adventure Course'?"

The day that the mage Priscilla happened upon our restaurant, she tilted her head curiously at the proposal that we presented to her.

Her reaction wasn't surprising.

After all, she'd come with the usual pamphlet in hand, curious to see how we lived our lives in The Giants' Kitchen.

But we hadn't treated her with hostility or entertained her in any way. Instead, we'd all lined up before her and presented our proposal.

"Recently we've decided to start a new enterprise…and we'd like to borrow a mage's power to do it."

That's right—it was a new business venture.

To tell the truth, we had been operating The Giants' Kitchen for a long time and had faced off against many travelers, but every time we battled, our resources were depleted.

Frankly, we hardly had anything left. Talk was circulating among the junior soldiers. People were saying "This isn't worth it" and "We object to this exploitation." There were even some who issued near-threats, like "I'll inform the labor union." Not that we have a labor union anyway.

With no better ideas, the captain had spoken up: "How about we just start a new business?"

And so we had devised the "Incredible Shrinking Adventure Course."

"Basically, we were looking for something more sustainable. So having guests shrink down to our small size works out well in several ways. If the guests are small, so are their stomachs, so they won't be able to consume as much, and the cost per guest will stay low."

We had approached the visiting mage with our proposal.

At the time, we didn't really know much about magic users, but we had figured that it should be pretty simple for one of them to shrink people down to our size.

"Hmm…"

Priscilla the mage had puzzled over the question with coquettish gestures. "I understand the situation. In short, you want me to provide you with potions that will make people and objects small; is that right? Well, I think I have something here…all right, now, where did I…"

As she talked, Priscilla pulled a potion bottle out of her bag.

Then she dribbled a little bit of it onto a bundle of paper (which was apparently called a "deck of cards").

Then something amazing happened. The bundle of paper shrank right before our eyes, until it was small enough to fit neatly into our hands. Priscilla presented the deck of cards to one of my comrades and explained that she was a mage who specialized in making potions.

It was clear that our proposal was a perfect match for her skills. However...

"But I've decided that I won't engage in such business any longer..." Priscilla frowned at our plan. Apparently, she had once been involved in certain dishonest enterprises but had since decided to turn her life around. She explained that when it came to her potions, she kept them on hand so she could give them out to people in need. I really wanted to ask if there were actually ever any circumstances where someone would need to shrink down to our size, but I decided to stay quiet for the time being instead.

"Well, please reconcile it somehow. We're counting on you!"

The captain bowed her head. I followed suit.

"If things remain as they are, our race will surely die out!" the captain told her tearfully. In her arms, she was cradling a girl on the verge of death—Liscia, one of our own.

Liscia had been suffering from a chronic lack of leaves, probably because customer traffic had been waning at The Giants' Kitchen lately. As a result, her mental state had become quite unstable.

"Oh...Captain...my Captain...when I die...wash me down the sink drain with some leaves..."

"Here, see for yourself! She's at death's door, isn't she?!"

By the way, Liscia had always been a bit of a drama queen.

But the mage Priscilla seemed shocked at Liscia's wretched state.

"...! My goodness!"

Liscia, of course, had always been wretched.

But Priscilla began to cry.

"I'll help you...I'll...I'll save all of you...!"

"Thank you." The captain grinned.

The most underhanded person of all had been with us the whole time.

After that, the mage Priscilla visited us almost every day. She came to have detailed meetings about the new business venture we were starting, of course, but more importantly, she had turned out to be more kindhearted than we'd ever imagined.

"This is called a BINGO game. You turn this clattering thing round and round, and punch holes in your card that match the numbers that fall out. When you complete a row, you win!"

Nearly every day, she brought some new plaything for us, who'd hardly had any decent entertainment. She would douse every new game in her shrinking potion and offer it to us.

She had all the benevolence of a goddess made flesh.

There were more than a few soldiers who said, "I want to marry that girl in the next life...," or something similar.

She had come to the cottage nearly every day to refine our business plan, and then, at long last, our scheme reached completion. Fortunately, since we had hung out the CLOSED FOR RENOVATIONS sign on the front door of The Giants' Kitchen, we hadn't had any customers in some time.

Then, that morning...

"All right, first thing tomorrow, we're switching over to the new business model."

We all agreed.

The details of our new enterprise were as follows:

There were three doors on the way into our restaurant. The first two would stay the same as always, directing people to remove their shoes and outerwear. But in front of the last door, we placed a bottled potion with DRINK ME! written on the side.

Customers who drank this potion would shrink until their bodies were the same size as ours. Then Priscilla would stuff them into a birdcage.

The record keeper, Acre, would be waiting inside the birdcage, and she would explain what was going on in the restaurant.

Then the customer would sneak out of the birdcage in order to recover the antidote from Priscilla. And essentially, along the way, my compatriots would each use their own methods to waste the traveler's time and get in their way.

After overcoming those obstacles, the customer would recover the antidote from Priscilla.

"Do you think I should also do something to block the traveler's way?"

Priscilla only appeared at the beginning of the scenario and then the rest of her role was spent sleeping.

The captain shook her head at the question.

"Don't worry. We'll put an end to everything while you're sleeping."

That seemed like a strange way to phrase it. An expression like that was just begging to be misunderstood.

The following day, we were busy with our final preparations.

"Bad news, Captain!"

The lookout was wearing a grim expression when she appeared before us with news.

"What is it?" The captain stayed quite calm.

Tears welling up in her eyes, the lookout answered, "Intruders have entered the restaurant! They took down the 'Closed for Renovations' sign and forced their way in!"

"What did you say?!"

It was an unforeseen situation. This was the first time that the giants had ever been so callous and rude as to break into a restaurant that was still setting up.

But even so, the captain kept her cool.

"All right, don't worry. We've been changing things around the restaurant, but the perfume should still be there in front of the last door like it always has been. There shouldn't be any problem with handling them like we always have."

However…

"About that…!"

The lookout shouted.

A brief but terrifying announcement.

"The potion! Is already! In place!"

The potion bottle with DRINK ME! written on it was already in its spot in front of the final door.

"Which one of you idiots left it in a place like that?!" the captain shouted furiously.

"Eh-heh-heh..." Liscia cackled.

"Why, yoooooouuuuuu!" The captain grabbed her by the collar.

Ultimately, we wound up rushing to entertain the travelers without being fully prepared.

○

"So in other words, The Giants' Kitchen is no longer the place where tiny women will treat customers with hostility and attack them, as it had been in the past... Is that what you're saying?"

"That's what I'm saying," Priscilla answered Linaria.

After Linaria had come crashing through the window, I had doused myself in the antidote potion and returned to my normal size. Linaria seemed to have finally regained her composure after I thoroughly explained the situation to her, and she confirmed the facts with Priscilla again.

"What a terrible ordeal that was..." Priscilla let out a sigh.

I think it went without saying that she had woken up in the worst possible way. That's because not only had she been awakened by a sudden pain on her face, but she had been confronted with a stranger, an extremely angry girl, pointing a wand at her and yelling, "Hurry up and return Alte to normal! I told you, put her back—don't you dare ignore me! What are you crying for? Stop messing around! If you don't do as I say, I'll break your fingers one by one!"

Fortunately, I had been there, right behind Linaria, and already back to my normal size, and I had managed to stop her from doing anything.

Linaria had glared at Priscilla before demanding to know what was going on.

Priscilla, on the other hand, had simply started crying.

After we went over the whole story again, and Priscilla and Linaria had gotten their composure back, I was finally able to tell Linaria what was going on with the restaurant.

I told her that the place had gone through a transformation since the pamphlets had originally been distributed. Linaria was quite despondent to hear of this state of affairs and just grumbled, "I see…"

Priscilla blew her nose loudly and responded to her. "It was awfully cruel of you to kick me out of nowhere…," she sobbed, still sitting on the floor.

"That was… I'm sorry about that." Linaria averted her eyes uneasily.

"Well, I suppose that just shows how magnificent my performance was!" A moment later, Priscilla was smiling as if nothing had happened. "So please, don't worry about it too much. And please don't apologize."

Certainly, her performance had been excellent. A bottle of eye drops was lying on the floor by her side.

Those were fake tears…

But the tiny women of The Giants' Kitchen had all clasped their hands and fixed their eyes upon her.

"She's a goddess…"

"There is a goddess among us…"

"Marry me…"

They worship her…

"…But I would have liked an explanation at least, if The Giants' Kitchen was changing," Linaria said.

"That was always our intention!" Priscilla told us. "After all, we were planning to start our new enterprise tomorrow. We were going to put up a new sign and everything."

As she said this, Priscilla showed us the newly made sign.

INCREDIBLE SHRINKING ADVENTURE COURSE

All the details were written there. By the way, the cost was one gold piece per person.

"It's priced quite fairly, oh-hoh-hoh!" Priscilla laughed.

In other words, if we had shown up the following day, the two of us would have apparently received a normal, hospitable welcome.

"......" I looked at Linaria.

"......" Linaria averted her eyes. "...I mean, I figured there would be a lot of people trying to hog the restaurant for themselves on opening day, so...," she squeaked out in an unusually frail voice.

"Well, that wasn't so bad if we consider it like a rehearsal for tomorrow. Though I am rather bruised... But what kind of relationship do the two of you have?"

What?

"What kind of relationship? What do you mean?" *What on earth is she talking about?* I wondered. "We're just ordinary friends..."

But Priscilla didn't seem convinced by my answer and tilted her head questioningly. "Is that so?"

She kept going.

"It's just, earlier, she was really quite angry—"

"Stop," Linaria interrupted.

"And she called you 'my Alte'—"

"Really, stop it." Linaria smacked her.

Huh?

Linaria had burst in so suddenly earlier that I hadn't really heard anything she said. I was very curious what this was all about.

"Did you really call me that?"

"I did not."

"What on earth does 'my Alte' even mean—"

"I never said that."

I got smacked, too.

It didn't hurt, but I thought I could see red creeping over Linaria's face, so I gave up on asking any more questions.

"My, my." Priscilla smiled broadly as she watched our exchange. "What a lovely thing to witness..."

"Your nose is bleeding."

"That's from when I got kicked in the head."

"Uh-huh...so you have brain damage..."

After that, Priscilla mumbled some nonsensical words for a little while—things like, "Two girls...how nice...," and so on. It was enough to make me anxious that she had lost a few marbles when Linaria had kicked her.

Ultimately...

They were starting their new business enterprise the next day. For the rest of that day, however, the three of us humans enjoyed very courteous entertainment from the tiny ladies of The Giants' Kitchen, in their own typical way.

This is something that we learned later on, but Priscilla was apparently attending a magic school in another country, and her school had a long holiday in the time between late winter and early spring, just like Latorita State University. That's why she had taken a part-time job at The Giants' Kitchen.

I see, I see.

"So you're wearing those clothes on purpose, in order to give off a villainous vibe?"

Apparently, her true identity was that of an ordinary student. She seemed like a decent person.

"Incorrect!" Priscilla replied enthusiastically. "I'm wearing this because I want to!"

"But isn't it hot?"

"It is hot! But I won't take it off!"

"......"

"Because this is who I am!"

......

She's probably just a weirdo after all.

○

Linaria and I left The Giants' Kitchen and mounted our brooms together.

Our history hunt had only just begun.

"I figured that it would be a strange restaurant, but…I never imagined that the whole thing would be one big practical joke…"

As I think back on the experience, there had been several points along the way when I ought to have been suspicious of what was going on, but I hadn't doubted a thing. I had just enjoyed my time in their little world.

I had a feeling that if I had been a little faster to realize that something was amiss, we would have never ended up meeting Priscilla, who seemed to have the wrong idea about us—

"Well, there was no helping it. They didn't have their sign out, after all. That's on them. Of course, it was partially on me, for throwing away the 'Closed for Renovations' sign, but…" She let out a sigh. "Sorry, Alte. This place was really different from what I expected."

For some reason, she sounded remorseful. But I didn't think she had anything to apologize for.

Besides…

I couldn't help saying that actually…

"It's my fault, too, for being so thickheaded."

"……" She stared fixedly at me. "Couldn't be helped. There's no cure for your thickheadedness."

"Huh…?"

I had been certain that she would contradict me, saying that I wasn't dull at all. But instead, she had spit poison in my face. If anything, she even looked a little peevish. She had her cheeks puffed out and everything.

"…Why are you mad?"

"I'm not mad."

"Yes you are, I can tell."

"I said I'm not mad!"

Linaria looked away in a huff.

For a short while, a quiet atmosphere filled the air around us.

Finally, I said, "…What country are we going to visit next?"

I cocked my head at Linaria, who was directing our history hunt. I couldn't tell yet where she was heading; I was just following her as she flew along on her broom.

I figured she must have a ton of places she wanted to go, since she was the one who had been going on endlessly about this trip.

She looked straight at me and asked, "Where do you want to go?"

Apparently, she also wasn't sure of our next destination.

Just like me.

We had only just started our brief journey together. I was sure that there were many more encounters and partings in our future. Perhaps the next place we visited would turn out to be exactly as Linaria had envisioned it, or maybe it would be someplace we never could have imagined.

So I answered.

"All right, I want to go to another place like The Giants' Kitchen."

That was all I said.

"…………?"

Linaria tilted her head.

She didn't seem to understand the meaning behind my words.

So I explained myself to the thickheaded girl.

I rephrased my request into something a bit more direct, and said:

"I just want to go somewhere fun."

Someplace that will blossom like a happy flower in my memories and make me smile whenever I think back on it. Whether it turns out to be how we expected or not. Somewhere amazing.

CHAPTER 3

The Resurrection Lily That Blooms in Solitude

This happened back when I was still an apprentice witch.

Before I became Saya the Charcoal Witch, I met a certain girl.

New recruits who have been accepted into the United Magic Association must first take lessons from Association witches for several months in order to become fully qualified members.

They study how to handle magic, hear explanations of the kinds of jobs the Association will commission them for, see examples of how the Association has resolved cases in the past, and learn basic skills for coping with situations until they are brought to resolution. Generally speaking, those several months are a period of intense learning in almost every field.

The girl and I first exchanged words around the beginning of this period. It really did happen by complete chance, but if I hadn't met her then, I doubt I would have ever spoken to her or made friends with her in my life.

I clearly remember the first day I ever spoke to her.

I was studying so I could work at the Association and training so I could become a witch at the same time, so after lectures were over for the day, I would stay behind at the branch office to learn magic from my instructor, Sheila.

I had repeated the same routine every day since arriving in the city, studying and training without a moment's rest. Accordingly, when it was time for me to go home for the day, the sun was always about to sink below the horizon. Studying made up the entirety of my daily existence.

I spotted the girl right as I was heading back to my lodging, exhausted from my demanding routine.

She had her purple hair tied up in a ponytail on one side of her head, and in spite of the bright color of her hair, there was a shadow hanging over her. She gave off the impression that she had left her mind behind somewhere. She always seemed to be searching for something. She seemed detached from reality. I had never seen her chatting pleasantly with anyone, not at the lectures and not during break times either.

Her name was Monica.

When I came upon her then, she seemed to be in a daze as always, crouching down silently, looking at a flower blooming by the side of the road.

The stem was growing straight up out of the ground. At the top was a red blossom, brighter than the setting sun, its petals spread out in a burst of color.

Monica was just staring at it, fixated.

Staring at the resurrection lily.

"Do you like those flowers?"

Even though I had never spoken to her, I recognized her face, so I stopped walking and addressed her.

"I do," she answered curtly, without even looking my way.

That was the first time that I heard her surprisingly clear and lovely voice.

"…What are you doing in a place like this?" I had stayed behind late because I had my special training to attend, but usually most of the new recruits dispersed around lunchtime. No one would have stayed at the branch office without a good reason.

"I was studying." As before, she answered without looking at me.

"Working overtime?"

"……" Monica nodded sharply.

Let me see now, can she really be so dense that she has to stay for extra lessons?

I had my doubts. I had known her for only a few weeks at that point, and this was our first time really meeting—actually, we had never even exchanged words before now—but I knew she always scored highly on our weekly exams.

Surely there's no need for her to work late? I thought. But immediately after I thought that, I realized something. *Maybe the reason she does so well on the exams is because she works late all the time? Wow, such a serious student.*

"I can't concentrate during the lectures, so I stay after class and study."

This time, she finally turned to look at me. Her purple eyes, the same color as her hair, seemed to sparkle in the evening sun.

"...Is it really that noisy during the lectures?"

The only people taking the lecture courses were the mages who were set to enter the Association as new recruits. We weren't actually students or anything; it was more like we were receiving training for the posts where we would each be working.

Sure enough, there were some girls who wouldn't think twice about quietly exchanging a few words with the person sitting next to them during the lectures, but that sort of chatting never got loud or anything. Truthfully, I had never noticed it or been bothered by it.

So I didn't really understand the meaning behind her words.

"......"

But she didn't offer any further explanation as I stood there with my head cocked. In her mind, she seemed to have decided that her conversation with me was over. Her eyes had already shifted from me back to the flower.

The resurrection lily.

In my homeland, it was regarded as a sinister, ominous flower.

Monica just kept staring at it.

"It's so beautiful, but there are people who hate it," she mumbled.

"That's the first time I've ever heard anyone call it beautiful."

"Oh?" As she spoke, she extended a hand toward the resurrection lily.

Oh my, uh-oh!

"Uh, you shouldn't touch that. It's poisonous."

She wouldn't actually be in any danger just from touching it, but it was the truth that the flower was toxic. I stopped her in somewhat of a panic.

In the bulb, and stem, and leaves, and even the vivid blossom—the resurrection lily had poison in every part of it. The whole thing was chock-full of poison. The reason why it was so hated was probably because it was toxic from root to tip, while having such a lovely appearance.

"…I see."

She withdrew her hand and stood up.

"It's so beautiful on the outside, but it does nothing but cause harm. Just like a human."

As before, I didn't really understand the meaning behind her words. Probably because I didn't think that the flower was especially beautiful in the first place.

Even so, I remember that day well, the day that I first spoke to Monica.

That's because her eyes, the eyes of the girl who had called the resurrection lily beautiful, were hopelessly steeped in sorrow.

○

I am a traveler who is at the same time affiliated with the United Magic Association, so my reason for hopping from country to country usually has something to do with my job.

Because of my experience traveling to so many places, or maybe because I am burdened with the unwieldy witch name of the Charcoal Witch, the Association often really takes advantage of me, and pressures me to accept jobs that the local registered witches don't want to do.

In the end, that was the main reason why I had come to this particular city on this particular day. A branch office agent of the United

Magic Association had contacted me with an appeal for assistance from a nearby city. So there I was, knocking at the gate.

Emadestrin, a Town Where People Live.

Deep in the gloomy forest, the city seemed to have been there since antiquity, long enough for thick ivy to creep up over the outer wall.

It was a plain, inconspicuous city, a place I probably never would have visited if I didn't have some business there.

As soon as I passed through the gate, a city official appeared before me. "You must be Lady Saya, the Charcoal Witch. We've been awaiting your arrival. Thank you very much for accepting this commission from our city."

Since I have a very petite frame, people often look puzzled when they first meet me. Many even doubt my abilities as a witch, despite my record handling various urgent matters. The official standing before me here, however, didn't react like that at all.

"Lady Saya, did you read the documents we sent concerning the incidents?"

Or maybe he simply had no interest in me personally. The official plowed straight through the formalities and, still wearing a stiff smile, immediately launched into the topic of the job at hand.

"...I read them on the way, mostly."

I nodded.

The Association had provided me with a dossier.

"Well then, my apologies for getting straight to it, but..." The official turned on his heel and urged me to follow. "I don't know whether your timing was good or bad, but this morning we had another incident, so I decided that I'd like to have a witch take a look at the scene. If you please."

I nodded and followed the official.

The simple, modest scenery of a city lined with old brick houses spread out before my eyes. It did not seem like the kind of town that would play host to any gruesome affairs or bloody incidents.

But, of course, that wasn't the case, which was why I had been summoned.

"It was apparently spotted this morning by a restaurant worker who was taking out the trash."

In a back alley.

The city official matter-of-factly explained the ghastly scene to me. The victim was an unmarried woman who had lived nearby. From the state of the remains, the conclusion was that she had died sometime the previous night.

"First of all, there can be no doubt that this was the work of the bloodthirsty serial killer who has been terrorizing our city. We've been seeing the same thing all across town. The killer leaves no external wounds and lays the victim's body out in an alleyway."

According to the request that was sent over to the United Magic Association, the killer had appeared about half a year earlier.

At first, everyone thought that victims were just collapsing in the street.

Then, one cold winter night…

Someone reported an awful smell outside their home, and when officials rushed over to investigate, they discovered a man was dead in a nearby alley. He was a homeless man who had been loitering around the area for a while, so no one had paid any attention when they saw him lying on the ground. No one had imagined that he was dead, and that had delayed the discovery. His body had no external wounds, his clothes weren't torn or ruffled, and there was a stolen bottle of alcohol lying nearby. From this evidence, city officials concluded that the man had simply collapsed and died.

But there was one peculiar thing about the scene: the position of his corpse.

His hands were tightly clasped, almost as if he were offering prayers to some deity, and he had died looking upward, face to the sky.

What on earth could he have been praying for?

Then, several days later, it became clear that this unfortunate homeless man had not, in fact, simply dropped dead all on his own.

Another corpse turned up in another alley.

This time, it was a young man in his thirties. He was a shopkeeper who had just opened a store nearby. A man who didn't seem to be having any difficulties in life. And there he lay, dead.

Just like the homeless man, he was found on his back, facing the sky, hands clasped as if in prayer.

The third victim was a teenage girl. She was an upstanding young woman who had never caused any trouble at home or at school, and she, too, was discovered in an alleyway, praying to the sky.

More bodies were discovered after that.

One victim was an elderly person. Another, a young person. Another, a man. A woman, too.

There was no connection to the weather, or the phases of the moon, and nothing seemed to connect the victims. The frequency of the murders was also scattered. Sometimes, two bodies would show up, one after another, and other times, half a month would go by without an incident. But over the past six months, too many people had been discovered lying discarded in back alleys.

"The only thing I can assume is that the killer is somehow mocking the customs of our city," the official spit coldly as he stared down at a woman's corpse praying to the dark but cloudless sky.

Here in Emadestrin, a Town Where People Live, the death of a human was regarded as the greatest of tragedies. Whether by murder or suicide, the act of snatching away a human life for any reason was considered the worst thing a person could do. So a series of murders like this was perhaps the most shocking thing imaginable.

So that was the sequence of events that led the city to request assistance from the United Magic Association.

However...

"...I thought there was a mage in this city who was affiliated with the United Magic Association. What's become of her?"

As soon as I'd gotten the request from this city, there had been no doubt about it. This city—Emadestrin, a Town Where People Live, was *her* hometown.

Monica.

The girl who always stayed late studying, who always got top marks on her exams and kept her grades up—she should have been working here.

That brilliant girl, much more capable than someone like me, was supposed to be here.

"......"

The official was silent for a while, then slowly nodded. "Yes...as you say, there is a mage in our city who is affiliated with the United Magic Association. I expect she is headed here as we speak. I believe you will be collaborating with her on this investigation."

"...Is that so?" I nodded.

Then the official added, "But listen, Lady Witch, please don't rely too heavily on her. We summoned you because it didn't seem like she could solve this on her own."

●

Walking through town, I could hear people mourning. I was not surprised, considering another gruesome incident had occurred.

I dropped my gaze to the brick-paved road as I walked, and all that reached my ears were voices full of disgust for the person who had let the culprit escape again.

"It's Monica."

"What is she doing in a place like this?"

"Even though she's a mage, she can't solve these crimes."

"What a useless mage she is..."

"She used to be much better, brilliant even…"

"At any rate, I don't suppose she's managed to find any clues today either."

I had been told that a witch was coming from the United Magic Association to help me today. Whether because of the difficulty of the case or my own incompetence in finding any leads, the city had apparently decided to enlist the help of someone else.

It was an unusual move for a place that didn't like to deal with outsiders, proof of the desperation and fear gripping the city in the wake of these serial murders.

"……"

I was sure that the city would have preferred to deal with the problem on its own rather than recruit outside help. However, I was apparently completely incapable of handling the matter.

When I'd first started working at the government office, there was no case I couldn't solve. But this case was different. Far from solving it, I couldn't even find any clues. So everyone thought I was totally incompetent.

Despite going to the trouble of taking myself to a foreign country and becoming an Association-affiliated mage, if I couldn't manage to produce some results in this case, then what good was the moon-shaped brooch on my chest anyway? That question had been hurled at me many times over these six months.

I didn't have any experience with people getting angry at me, so each time I just answered, "I'll get it right next time."

But the city had apparently finally given up on me.

The result was an appeal for assistance.

I was almost certainly finished here.

"Tomorrow, a witch is coming from the head office of the United Magic Association to help us. You will act as her assistant."

When I had been informed of that the day before, I finally understood. I knew that there wouldn't be a next case, not for me, not if I couldn't solve this one.

©Azure

Pretending not to hear the scathing criticism that people hurled at me freely, I turned a corner and ducked into a back alley.

I didn't want to meet her.

I would know what she thought of me as soon as I saw her, so I really, really didn't want to.

After all, any witch from the Association would surely ridicule me, just like the people of this city.

I would be exposed as a pathetic mage who had accomplished nothing despite dressing myself in a robe—the formal uniform.

So I really didn't want to meet her.

"……"

From the darkness of the alley, the witch turned to look at me.

But—

What I saw on her face was not disgust or scornful laughter.

Instead, there was joy and affection.

"…Monica."

She called my name.

I saw a very familiar face before me.

"…Saya."

My one and only friend was standing there.

○

I remember it like it was yesterday.

"Basically, the United Magic Association gets requests to solve cases and incidents that have something to do with magic, and sometimes we get called in when it's still unclear whether the situation was originally caused by a mage or not. That's my area of responsibility. Nice to meet you all."

My teacher, Sheila, was also a lecturer for the new recruits.

Her specific area of responsibility was murder cases.

She spoke matter-of-factly, standing at the lectern in front of the new-recruit mages, who were seated in rows of chairs.

"You could say that murder cases are the most troublesome among all the commissions that the United Magic Association receives. Because at the time the request is made, we don't even know whether the culprit is a mage or not, you see?"

Mm-hmm, I see. I nodded with a know-it-all look on my face.

"By the way, what do you think is the first thing we have to do when we get a request to work on a murder case? Saya."

"Huh? Why are you calling on me?"

"You were nodding along."

"……"

I shouldn't have had that know-it-all look on… She surprised me with a question, and I don't know the answer… This is the first lecture…

I started to panic under Sheila's fixed gaze. But she kept staring. The look in her eyes was threatening—*Hurry up and answer, hey, if you can't answer, it must mean you don't know*—and grew ever sharper. I kept on panicking. Before long, my eyes filled with tears. I was done for.

Eventually, a pen on my desk started to rattle around. At first, I thought that my own trembling was shaking the desk, but when the pen floated up in the air and started to scrawl out letters, I realized that it was moving because of magic.

The pen began writing words in thin air.

"…'Learn about the area'?"

I read out exactly what it wrote, and Sheila nodded.

"That's right. When an incident has occurred, the most important thing to do first is to learn about the region where the incident took place. For example, if a series of murders have occurred in a country where there are no magic users, most of the time, the culprit is probably not a mage. That's because a mage would stand out in a place without any other mages. The opposite is also true. When it comes to murder cases—especially serial murders—it's rare that a visitor is the one doing the killing. It's best to think of the culprit as someone who's local."

Continuing from there, Sheila launched into her lecture proper.

The pen that had written words on its own fell with a clatter onto my notebook. Someone had apparently given me a helping hand.

Sitting in the seat next to me was Monica.

"......" She sneakily tucked away her wand so that I wouldn't see it. But the truth was obvious. I leaned over and whispered into her ear quietly enough that no one else could hear.

"...Did you prepare for the lesson?"

"More or less," she said with a nod.

"Thank you for helping me."

"Whatever." She immediately turned away.

Generally, that's about how it went with her. Somehow, she and I started talking to each other after that and started doing things together, too.

"Monica! Want to eat lunch together?"

"Whatever."

"That means we can eat together, right? I get it!"

After that, we started eating lunch together regularly.

"Monica! It's break time; do you want to chat?"

"Whatever."

"That means you do, right? I get it! By the way, what do you do on the weekends?"

"Nothing."

She and I also started spending our breaks together.

"Monica, where are you from?"

"Emadestrin, a Town Where People Live."

"When our training period is over, will you go back to your hometown to get a job?"

"I have no plans to return."

"Oh, so you'll work in some other country or something?"

"I haven't thought about it."

"......"

"......"

Coincidentally, we also started heading home together more frequently.
......

Actually, it's possible that I was just developing a one-sided connection with her.

But just because she didn't particularly want to talk to anyone, that didn't mean that she had to be alone. And just because she wasn't inclined to make friends with anyone, that didn't mean that she had to just stare out the window.

As time passed, her attitude gradually softened up.

"Monica, what do you do on the weekends?"

"I get up, read a book, study, and go to bed. In short, I do nothing," she answered.

"Is that so…?" I struggled to respond.

About a month had gone by since we started taking courses at the United Magic Association, and I had kept up with both my lectures and my training to become a witch, every day without pause, whether it was a weekday or a weekend. But suddenly, I had an actual break coming up, for the first time in a long while.

My teacher Sheila had received a request for aid from a nearby country. She'd told me, along with a snarky comment about it being "a real pain in the ass," that we would be taking a break from training that weekend. In other words, since my training plans for the weekend were now wiped clean, and an unexpected gap had suddenly opened in my normally jam-packed schedule.

So since this was such a rare occurrence, I thought I might try walking around someplace other than the Magic Association branch campus, but…it occurred to me that Monica was in the same boat as me, and only ever went between her lodgings and the branch campus and back again.

"…I don't normally do anything on the weekends, but if I do happen to have some free time, I go out into town and wander around." Surprisingly, Monica seemed to read my mind, and suggested, "…If you want to go sightseeing around town, I'll go with you."

I was delighted.

Both with the suggestion itself, and the fact that Monica had proposed something like that, when she was always so cold.

"All right, then, would you please show me around a bit?"

So I took her up on her offer.

And I depended on her in the days after that as well.

She wore a grumpy expression, but she accepted my request.

She might be cold, but she's a good person.

After we'd turned the corpse in the alley over to the custody of the city's medical experts, Monica and I headed for city hall.

There didn't seem to be a branch office of the United Magic Association here, and in its absence, the government apparently handled cases and incidents related to magic in a department in city hall.

Well, I say "department," but...

"Basically, I alone am responsible for dealing with all cases and incidents related to magic. As you can see."

The room I was shown to contained a sofa for receiving visitors and a desk scattered with papers. There were apparently quite a few magic users in the city, but it didn't seem like any of them were keen on working for the government.

"Most mages work at the hospital... It's rare for one of us to take this kind of employment."

Apparently, Monica had been sleeping in her office because there were blankets on the sofa and a pile of discarded clothes nearby. For a room in a government building, it had a real lived-in feel.

"...Can you manage the job on your own?"

"I could, at least until these past six months."

Huh? Reeeally?

I couldn't help narrowing my eyes intently, given the state of the room...

"They told me I could use the office however I wanted..."

Monica averted her eyes, seeming a little ashamed under my gaze.

"…Are you doing all right? Have you been sleeping?"

"Not much lately."

The incidents had probably cut into her sleeping time.

"I hope the incidents are over soon."

"No kidding." Monica yawned once, then sat down on the sofa. "Please." She urged me to sit, too. I sat down facing her.

Then, taking another long, hard look at me, she said, "But to think the witch they sent us turned out to be you. What a surprise!"

The fact that she didn't actually look all that surprised was probably because she had never been very expressive. She didn't seem to have changed a bit from when we were new recruits.

"I was surprised, too. I heard that a request for aid had come in from your hometown, so—"

I had figured the situation must really be dire if Monica couldn't deal with it. She was an excellent mage, much more talented than someone like me.

She was certainly more cut out for the work than stumpy little Saya, even if I did carry the title of "witch."

"…………" After a very solemn silence, Monica said, "…It's a case that I just couldn't solve." She averted her eyes.

"I've already read the details in the files they sent over. Seems like a really troublesome serial murderer, huh?"

"If it wasn't, I wouldn't have called for backup."

I knew we had learned some general information about murder cases and the strategies for solving them in our training courses when she and I were new recruits, but even so, this case was daunting.

Speaking boldly and honestly, I hadn't been enthusiastic about coming to this city, both because it was Monica's hometown and because I had had a hunch that this case would be difficult to untangle.

"What do we do now?" Monica tilted her head inquisitively.

"Well, we're in a situation with no clues, but…still, we know what we have to do."

"…What's that?"

Let's recall what we learned in our lectures. When we come across a murder case, as members of the United Magic Association, we know what the first thing to do is.

Namely, we must learn about the area.

In other words…

"Would you please show me around town a little?"

●

Considering I was currently quite unpopular around town, I had hoped to avoid walking around with Saya. But since she had asked, I figured it couldn't be helped.

I took her to many places throughout the city.

We started with the spot where the first incident had taken place. It was an ordinary back alley, sandwiched between two houses. Our next stop was the alley near the restaurant. Then an alley near the bakery. After that, another alley between houses. And another alley. Then we went to an alley, and another alley after that.

"What's up with all the alleys?!" After walking through more than ten of them, Saya expressed her frustration at yet another alley. "Jeez!"

I shook my head and answered simply, "The incidents all happened in places like this."

"Are there no places we could visit other than the crime scenes?"

If we were going to follow what we learned when we were new recruits, we needed to tour the city in order to get to know the area. I knew that was why she'd asked me to show her around town. However…

"This tour has been back-alley-focused, but you should have gotten a clear idea of the atmosphere of the city," I said. "Our city isn't an especially dangerous place, you see. And there are a fair number of mages, but it's mostly non–magic users."

"……" As Saya listened to what I was saying, she stared at the people coming and going down the main thoroughfare that was visible from the darkness of the alley. "But the wealth disparity is pretty extreme, huh?"

Walking out there in the sunlight were the city's valued citizens.

Saya had probably noticed the disparity while we were walking through town, and she was exactly right.

"It's probably more accurate to say that it's easy for mages to become rich."

Every one of the mages mixed into the crowd looked like they were dressed in resplendent fashion. Their triangular hats were decorated with golden ornaments, and some wore necklaces of jewels on their chests. It was obvious they had more money than they knew what to do with.

But that didn't seem out of place to me. It was only natural that mages had an easier time making money.

Because there are lots of things that mages can do better.

And there are some things that only mages can do.

So it was unavoidable.

"...So are there no places we could visit other than the crime scenes?" Saya was still staring at the road.

I nodded. "Just one place."

The place where most of the mages living in the city worked. The hospital.

The hospital was the only place that treated injuries and illnesses and developed new medicines. It was also where corpses were taken for autopsy. In many ways, the hospital was the heart of the city.

Most mages worked there, to help the citizens of Emadestrin. They were indispensable to the community, and I had no doubt that the people placed more confidence in them than in someone like me.

At the same time, I knew that the mages at the hospital were less than pleased every time I came in with the fresh corpse of yet another murder victim.

So if I'd had any way to refuse, I would have avoided taking Saya there at all.

"Take me there, please." But she turned around and smiled at me.

"Let's hurry up and finish our work for the day, and then go get something good to eat together!"

I felt my chest tighten.

The largest, oldest building in Emadestrin, a Town Where People Live, was the hospital. There wasn't even any need for me to show Saya the way. I just said, "That's the hospital over there," and started walking, with her accompanying me. We didn't even talk on the way, and it didn't take much time before we arrived.

When we went inside, a doctor rushed over to us as soon as she saw me. "We finished the autopsy," she said icily.

She was the physician in charge of autopsies, Frauze.

The doctor led the two of us to the morgue. "Though I doubt you'll figure anything out by seeing it," Frauze whispered bitterly, so that Saya wouldn't hear, and then she showed us the body of a girl who had collapsed in an alleyway.

"As you can see, there are no external wounds. And no toxic substances were detected. It's likely that healing magic was used on her after she was killed. There were no clues left behind on this corpse."

"......" Saya, who had stayed about three steps behind me ever since we arrived at the hospital, frowned and looked away from the body. "In other words, it fits the motive of the murderer in question?"

For some reason, her voice sounded pained. It was obvious that she was not used to looking at dead bodies, and her breathing had become a little ragged, as if she had forgotten how to breathe.

"That's correct." Frauze nodded. "She was most likely killed in her sleep, and then her body was restored to its normal state... It's a small mercy that she was able to meet her end without suffering."

The killer's victims were abandoned in back alleys, looking like beautiful dolls that had never had life in them to begin with. No matter how well the culprit fixed up the corpses, even if they knit every wound, it didn't change the fact that the victims would never return to life.

"I wonder why the culprit leaves the bodies in alleyways? If killing people is the goal, then it seems like going to all the trouble of fixing them up just to dump them outside would be a big waste of effort."

Frauze shook her head at Saya's question. "My job is examining the corpses. I really have no idea."

"……"

"I shall cooperate with you to the best of my ability, so that this case can be solved as promptly as possible." As she spoke, Frauze covered the body up with a sheet. "However, aside from the fact that the perpetrator was the same killer as before, there is nothing else I can learn from this corpse. I'm terribly sorry that I can't be of more assistance…"

Then she bowed once politely and, in a detached, formal tone, said stiffly, "Again, you have our full cooperation, that you may solve these cases as quickly as possible."

This came as no surprise to me. It would have been nice if the most recent body had provided any clues, but I'd known it was a long shot. Our investigation was immediately at a standstill.

"No clues again, huh…? I thought maybe we would learn something by looking at the body, but…"

Walking briskly in front of me, Saya was trying to get out of the hospital quickly.

If there weren't any clues, then we no longer had any business there.

"Let's go back to city hall. There's nothing for us here."

"…You're right."

I couldn't stand the hospital. I had never wanted to go there in the first place, partially because I knew that there wouldn't be any clues for us, but that wasn't the only reason I had been so reluctant.

The real reason I hated the hospital was the awful sense of despair that seemed to envelop the place.

"…This is the infirmary, isn't it?" As Saya walked down the hallway, she peered into the rooms one by one.

Inside were rows of feeble patients laid out on cots.

"Lycoris Disease."

"...What?"

"It's an illness that has been spreading through our city for some time," I explained from behind her. "People get infected without knowing it, and once the illness takes hold, the first symptom to appear is a high fever. When the fever dies down, next they lose the ability to move, then gradually lose all control over their bodies, lose consciousness, and then finally, they fall into a vegetative state."

"......"

"Even when we're able to detect it early, before fever symptoms start to show, we haven't been able to slow the progression of the disease."

By the time the illness was detected in a patient's body, they were faced with an awful choice. They could either leave the city and die someplace else, or they could die here after being burdened with immense medical expenses. But in order to leave the city, they had to deal with equally immense departure costs. In the end, normal people without any money had little choice but to stay.

However, taking a life in any capacity was a serious crime in the city. That applied to euthanasia as well. Even stopping the administration of medication to someone who was riddled with disease and possibly unconscious was considered no different than premeditated murder.

For that reason, the mages working at the hospital could not stop treating these patients. And that's why despair ran rampant through the place.

"...In other words, as soon as someone contracts the disease, their grim fate is sealed?"

"Right." I nodded. "All they can do is lie in bed and endure the suffering until they die."

It was a miserable thought, but there was nothing anyone could do. So the mages continued their treatments, prolonging the lives of people who were never going to recover.

I couldn't stand this place.

Because the contradictions of this city were on display at every turn.

"Oh, Monica came by, huh?"

"She must be investigating another case."

"What an unpleasant sight she is."

"She can't do anything."

Besides that, voices criticizing my incompetence echoed freely down the halls.

"She'll never live up to her father's legacy, I guess," someone uttered.

I stopped in my tracks and turned around, but nobody was looking my way. As if they had all conspired together, everyone had their back to me and was walking away.

"…What's wrong, Monica?"

"…No, it's nothing."

I shook my head and followed Saya out.

At least I could consider it a silver lining that the voices hadn't seemed to reach Saya's ears.

Saya and I stuck together for a while even after I'd finished showing her around.

"Say, Monica? Let's interview witnesses for the investigation this afternoon!"

"…I don't think we're going to find any clues, though."

"Come on, don't say that!"

Saya dragged me outside, and we started to interview various people. From afternoon until night, we wandered around town, even though I knew perfectly well that it wouldn't yield any results no matter how long we kept at it, since I had already long since investigated whether or not there were any eyewitnesses among the citizens.

Yet Saya walked around town the following day, and the day after that, pulling me along behind her.

Nearly every day, she would visit various places with me, buy some snacks, go watch a show, and do other, similar leisure activities. Then she would conduct some interviews about the incidents almost as an afterthought.

"All right, Monica, where should we go next?" Saya smiled at me as we walked through a crowd. She was carrying an armful of bread that she had purchased at a nearby street stall.

"...You've got to be kidding?"

To start with, the place that we were visiting now was a main street that had nothing at all to do with the incidents. It was an utterly inappropriate place to conduct witness interviews, and it was obvious that coming here was a wasted effort.

There was no meaning to it at all.

"I'm doing my job, more or less," Saya said to me as I frowned suspiciously at her. "I've come to a place that has nothing to do with the incidents, and I'm watching the reactions of the townspeople."

"...For what purpose?" I tilted my head.

Saya answered matter-of-factly, "Humans are selfish creatures, so no matter how many others are suffering, they can ignore it as long as it's happening somewhere else." Pressing a piece of bread into my hands, she continued, "And at least around here, there aren't that many people who are upset with you. If anything, there are too many people around to tell who might hate you, right, Monica?" Saya said, as if it was a matter of course.

I thought I had managed to keep my troubles hidden from her, but she had obviously guessed what was going on with no difficulty.

"............" So I was surprised. "You noticed?"

I felt just like she had read my mind.

"I knew right away. You had such a pained look on your face."

"...I thought I had on the same expression as I always do, but—"

"That's not what it looked like to me, not at all."

"Oh?"

"No. When someone is in pain, sometimes it's all they can think about. They don't have the energy to think about anything else." Saya took another bite of bread, swallowed it, and continued, "You may think you're acting normally, but everyone else can see that that's not true at all."

"............"

"When you're having a tough time, the best thing to do is to cast aside everything in your head and wander around absentmindedly in an unfamiliar place, thinking about nothing. So now that we're somewhere that has nothing to do with the incidents, will you wander awhile like this with me?"

It seemed like I was even more exhausted than I had realized.

The bread that Saya had given to me was unbelievably delicious. As it passed my lips and dropped into my empty belly, I remembered that I had hardly eaten anything in the past few days.

"It's good, right? Well, it is bread that I bought, after all!"

Bossy Saya was there by my side, spouting logic that I hardly understood.

I smiled.

"That's what I like about you."

"Aw, I'm blushing."

I wanted this peaceful time to continue forever, just like this.

But...

"Saya, don't forget that we have a mission... We have to solve this case as quickly as possible."

"There's no problem there," snorted the bossy Saya proudly. "After all, visiting a place that has no connection to the incidents is also the thing to do when an investigation gets tough."

Then she pointed to the edge of the street.

This was a place with lots of pedestrian traffic, so there were all sorts of folks coming and going. People shopping. The fragrance of delicious-smelling food. Carts carrying heavy loads. Adults on their way to work. Mages buying snacks. People passing up and down the street on all sorts of business.

We also noticed a homeless man on the side of the broad street, someone who had nowhere else to go. Saya was pointing at the man, who I could see was sitting on a wooden crate, begging for money from passersby.

"If I remember correctly, the first victim was a homeless man, right?" She looked excited as she gazed at the man by the side of the road. "And look, the pose that he's in, doesn't it resemble the way that all the victims were praying?"

In other words, she seemed to have discovered a connection between the incidents and this homeless man, who was begging for money.

I let out a sigh.

"...He's not praying."

"Hm? Then what is that pose?"

I answered, "He's begging for salvation."

Up until now, I had never asked anyone for help, or expected anything from anyone.

I had always believed that it was pointless to do so.

My mother left us before I was old enough to understand, and my father, who was a doctor, worked late every night, so I was always left at home alone. Even when my father did come home, all he did was drink. I had no memories of playing with my father when I was young.

I always did all the cooking and housework by myself. Other adults would frown and say, "Poor thing," as they watched me do the shopping when I was a child, not yet ten years old. But I knew perfectly well that my father loved me from the bottom of his heart. Much more than the strangers who just pitied me from a distance. He loved me deeply.

From the time I was very small, my father wanted to get me out of the city.

"You're a magical genius," he told me. "It would be a waste for you to use your powers in a narrow-minded place like this."

He said such things to me often. Eventually I found myself wanting to meet my father's expectations and get out of the city.

So I worked hard, harder than anyone else. All the other kids who had been born into magical families aspired to become local doctors, but I alone began to study to join the United Magic Association.

Everyone looked at me like I was some kind of freak. Some people thought I was just eccentric, and other people looked down on me, calling me my father's puppet.

Despite all that, I continued studying, trying to live up to my father's expectations.

I easily passed my mage exams (either because I studied so hard, or maybe just because nobody else in my hometown was interested in working for the United Magic Association) and was all ready to leave the city.

My father paid the unbelievably expensive departure costs for me, and I set off. He'd been too busy with work to see me off in person. The last words I ever exchanged with him were earlier the day of my departure, when he'd suddenly told me, "Don't ever come back here."

That was the only thing he ever said to me that resembled a farewell.

In his eyes as he looked at me then, I could see his feelings for my mother, whose face I had never known.

In truth, I had always wanted to save lives, just like my father. But I had never admitted it out loud.

I had known everything since I was young.

I had known, better than anyone, that my father hoped I wouldn't live my life as he had.

And yet in the end, I had returned to the city.

Once I was accepted into the United Magic Association, I was supposed to spend the first few months attending lectures with all the other new recruits.

Personally, I thought it would be a waste of time.

All my fellow students were confident, outgoing girls, and when lessons were over, they would stand around the lecture hall asking each other if they wanted to go get something to eat or hang out elsewhere. It seemed like they were only interested in having a good time.

Rather than concern themselves with their future responsibilities, all they worried about was having fun and goofing off when they should have been studying. From what I could see, there was only one other girl there who was earnestly trying to learn anything.

"I will definitely become a witch, I will definitely become a witch, I will become a witch, I will become a witch, I will become a witch, I will become a witch, I will become a witch, I will become a witch…"

She was the odd one out, mumbling her mantra in the seat next to mine.

"…………"

Her face was stiff with nervousness when she first introduced herself and told me her name was Saya. There was definitely something strange about her. She said she wanted to work with the Association while traveling.

Most of the new recruits in our class were planning to return to their hometowns as soon as their training was over, so that they could work for their local branch offices. Someone like Saya, who wasn't planning to go back home, really stood out.

She and I had that in common.

Maybe that was why I noticed her. Every day, she showed up to class looking like she was at death's door, and during breaks she just studied. She didn't speak to anyone. Once the lectures for the day had ended, she would immediately run off somewhere. There were times that other girls attempted to invite her to go hang out, but in the end, she barely seemed to acknowledge them. Eventually, everyone began to think of her as an oddball, but she didn't seem to even notice.

The other mages back in my hometown had looked at me the same way. Maybe that explained the strange affinity I felt for her.

I decided at some point that I would like to try to talk to her sometime. But even though I was interested, I hadn't actually spoken to anyone either, and I strongly doubted that I would ever get the chance.

Even now, I remember our first conversation quite well. We ran into each other on the way home from studying.

※   ※   ※

From that day on—actually, from the next day on—she made a point to come talk to me during every break and after every lecture. Probably because I had caught her attention during class.

When she did, I gave her only cold, short responses. Which was the opposite of how I really felt.

When other girls approached me, they didn't even try to hide their intentions. They were only interested because I was a good student. So it took me a long time to let my guard down.

Even so, Saya kept talking to me.

I was so happy.

Eventually, she and I became friends.

"And then, see, the witch who helped me out back then, Elaina is her name, she's generally a pretty good person, and—"

Saya often talked about the witch who'd rescued her.

Really, really often.

Enough that I was completely sick of hearing about her.

"...I've heard this story ten times already."

"Great, I'll tell you a hundred more times!"

"……"

According to Saya, this Elaina person was the witch who had inspired her to become a witch herself.

Even though I made terribly bored faces at Saya whenever she repeated the same stories over and over, I really felt jealous that she knew a witch who had had such an influence on her.

I thought about how nice it would be to mean that much to someone.

Saya and I talked about a lot during that time together, but none of it was worth noting. Our time together as students was not particularly exciting.

However, I loved the time that I spent with Saya. Even though I always wore a sullen expression, I loved hearing her tell me about herself, and I loved every minute that she spent with me.

We began walking home together after lectures each day.

"She's as merciless as ever..."

Miss Sheila, Saya's teacher, must have been very strict, because Saya was always completely exhausted. I didn't know why she put up with it, maybe because of how badly she wanted to become a witch, or because she wanted to catch up with Elaina or whoever. Whatever the case, Saya was completely absorbed in her training. She certainly didn't balk at hard work. Compared to the other girls, who were just going through the motions of taking the lectures, Saya seemed much engaged.

"...Sorry to hear that. If you'd like, we could go get something to eat."

"Yes, please!"

Saya was the kind of girl whose intentions were always written plainly on her face. As soon as I looked at her, I could tell what she was thinking. She did not seem to have a single underhanded bone in her body. If she was happy, she smiled broadly; if she was sad, she frowned; and if she felt hungry, you could read it on her face.

She always said what was really on her mind, and I felt like I could trust her more than anyone else. That was why we could spend time together.

"You're a really honest person, aren't you?"

"Well, there's no reason to lie, is there? I'm hungry!" Saya answered coolly. She added, "Actually, I lied once a long time ago, but I got found out."

"By Elaina, right? I know."

"Did I tell you about this already?"

"Only about ten times or so."

"Well, I'll just have to tell you a hundred times, then!"

"Please don't. My ears will fall off."

Saya was always repeating the stories she told me about herself.

One day during a break, as she was animatedly telling me some trivial tale, I'd asked her for the first and only time: "...Why do you tell me these stories about yourself?"

Saya had looked at me with a curious expression, then, as expected, answered me truthfully, "Hm? Isn't it normal to want your friends to know more about you?"

"…………"

I wondered just how normal that was.

I had never made a friend before, I had never wanted anyone to know about me, and I had never met anyone whom I cared to get to know.

In my case…

I had also never been able to trust anyone else.

"…And is it normal to accept your friends for who they are?"

Even I had to wonder what I was asking. I would have been utterly bewildered if anyone had suddenly asked me such a thing.

Saya tilted her head curiously. I could tell that she was wondering what I was getting at. But then she laughed easily and said, "Well, I'm not sure, but I think that would be a normal thing to do, right?"

Of course, these words, too, contained no lies, only her true feelings.

"…………"

That was when a foolish thought came to me. I thought that maybe, if anyone could understand me, it would be Saya. That this girl in front of me might somehow choose to stay with me even after she knew about my past.

And so…

"The thing is, I…," I started to tell her.

To tell her my truth.

The truth about me.

But…

"Break's over. Lecture's starting, so take your seats."

…I had really bad timing. As soon as I opened my mouth to speak, Miss Sheila casually strolled through the door to the lecture hall.

"Ah! Sorry! We'll talk later!" Saya hurriedly returned to her own seat. She seemed particularly intimidated by her teacher.

In the end, I didn't get the chance to tell her my secret.

I kept that secret, which I had never told anyone, not even my father, hidden in my heart, as the lecture began.

○

"Generally speaking, serial killers can be divided into two criminal categories."

My teacher Sheila was giving a lecture about how serial killers can be sorted into the predatory *hunter* type and the *impulsive* type.

"One category contains the people who kill because they enjoy it. These are typically intelligent people who understand that murder flies in the face of morality. Fundamentally, this variety of killer is smart, and proficient at communicating with others. Often both of their parents are alive and well, and they were born into the upper social classes. Killers with these characteristics frequently think of murder as a hobby. In other words, these are the hunters."

Sheila continued, "But the other major type of killer is the opposite of the hunter. They don't actually enjoy killing, and they're not capable of understanding that it is wrong. Typically, killers of this type are less intellectual and have difficulty communicating with other people. Oftentimes they have only one parent. Poverty may also be a factor. Killers with these characteristics often suffer from visual and auditory hallucinations, and that suffering leads them to commit murder. In short, to these *impulsive* types, killing people is simply a means to an end…but there are those serial killers who do not fit either of these classifications. Do you know why that might be? Monica?"

Sheila suddenly called on Monica, but Monica didn't look worried at all. With a very cool expression, she answered, "Because those people likely possess characteristics of both classifications."

Sheila nodded. Monica had apparently answered correctly.

"That's right. And this type of serial killer is considered to be even more difficult to catch. *Hunters* tend to be very selective about their prey. Most of them also use weapons that they have prepared beforehand, so if you base your investigation on the victims and the tools used to kill them, it's easy to narrow down a suspect. *Impulsive* killers aren't too picky and kill at random—on impulse—but since they often improvise weapons and tend to make a mess of the crime scene, they usually leave plenty of physical evidence, and you can narrow down a suspect if you start your investigation from the scene of the crime. But people who have both types of characteristics are a different story."

Sheila explained that, basically, they leave no evidence behind at the scene, and it's extremely difficult to figure out how they choose their victims.

"Killers who fall outside the two major categories are almost impossible to profile. If you find yourself on the trail of one of those, you can expect a difficult investigation."

She must have confronted such a killer in the past. Sheila stood in front of the lectern, shrugged her shoulders, and let out a sigh.

"It might take you a long time to catch them, which can sometimes lead the community you're working in to doubt your abilities. This can be…difficult."

At the time, Sheila had warned us, almost like a threat—

"You'd better be prepared if you ever have to deal with that type of killer."

And then we found out that it really was just like Sheila had said.

All that I knew, after entering this city and investigating for several days, was that the culprit left no clues to speak of. The killer appeared out of nowhere, committed the murder, and disappeared without leaving behind any evidence. We didn't even know the killer's age or gender, let alone any defining characteristics, and all we had done was waste precious time.

Monica and I had started going on patrol together, hoping to at least prevent any more murders from occurring. Even though the city's soldiers were supposed to be keeping watch, we felt that only mages like us were fit to take on another mage, so with Monica by my side, I walked around the city every night until it was late.

A week passed.

As always, there were no developments in our investigation.

And so the curtain fell on another day, free of death.

How pleasant it would be if we could just spend our time like this. How joyous if things would stay like this, with no murders.

"So what it comes down to is that a serial killer who is both *impulsive* and a *hunter* is someone who is very intelligent yet feels compelled to kill people—is that what it means?"

"If they possess characteristics of both types, then I think that's what it means."

"I wonder why they have to kill people."

"Who knows?" Monica's voice was cold. "I wonder why, myself."

It wasn't something I often heard Monica say. Ordinarily, Monica just knew things; her knowledge seemed boundless. For instance, during our lessons, whenever there had been something I hadn't been able to understand, she had always quickly explained things for me.

It always seemed like there was nothing that Monica didn't know.

I smiled at her. "Monica, where should we go tomorrow?"

As I looked at her from the side, her expression seemed wracked with distress.

I had been thinking that she must be wearing herself out again, and that we ought to go somewhere to relax.

I wanted to see Monica smile again, even just a little.

But she seemed to see right through me and shook her head.

"We have work tomorrow, too. I'm not going anywhere unrelated to the case, like we did before."

"But—"

"I'm not going."

Then she came to a sudden halt.

"……"

A moment later, I stopped, too. When I turned around, I saw Monica standing beneath a streetlight, hanging her head.

She stood in the light, but her expression was dark, as if she might dissolve into the shadows at any moment.

I spoke to her.

"…All right, at the very least, if something's bothering you, won't you discuss it with me? You're my friend, Monica. Why are you suffering alone? Why won't you tell me anything? Something is causing you pain, isn't it? So why…?"

Why are you hanging your head like that?

As soon as I saw her face, I knew the answer.

No matter how unreadable her expression was, or how little her emotions fluctuated, I knew. It had been many years since we last met, but I had seen Monica make a face like that once during the time we'd spent together as new recruits.

So when I saw it, I knew.

I'd known as soon as I'd arrived in this city and saw Monica again.

She was being tormented by some intractable problem.

I stared her straight in the face.

But Monica averted her eyes.

"Let's work separately from tomorrow on. We shouldn't be together."

"…No way. We're sticking together."

"Why?"

"……" I answered, "I can't let you go off on your own, Monica. In your state, if you're by yourself, you might get attacked by the killer—"

"I'm fine. I won't get attacked."

"But…"

"Or are you saying that because you'll be at a disadvantage if you let me go off on my own?"

"……"

Monica looked at me with eyes that felt like they were looking right through me, and I couldn't help averting my gaze.

It was as if my whole world had gone dark. From somewhere on the edges of my perception, I heard a sigh, and then a sorrowful voice, filled with disappointment.

"You're not how you used to be anymore, are you?"

●

After the day's lectures were over…

Saya had her witch training and I stayed behind to study, so we would often each be heading home at the same time, and as the days of lectures wore on, we walked home together more often.

On the day in question, we were walking down the road, side by side, as the sun set.

"Come to think of it, what were you trying to tell me this afternoon?"

As I was staring at a resurrection lily blooming along the side of the road, Saya suddenly intruded on my field of vision, her head tilting to the side inquisitively.

I immediately understood that she wanted to know the rest of what I had been about to say before Sheila had started her lecture.

But I was too embarrassed to say it again.

"What do you mean?" I feigned ignorance.

"You were about to tell me something, weren't you? What was it that you wanted to say?"

"Nothing in particular."

"Huh? You're lying. You were definitely going to tell me something. What was it? Love troubles?"

"No."

"All right, what then?"

"I told you, nothing in particular."

"…Hmm, is that so?" Based on her personality, I was on my guard, expecting Saya to try to draw the secret out of me by force, if necessary. But she backed off immediately. "Well, if you don't want to tell me, that's fine, but…"

But she continued.

"...If you do want to tell me, don't hold back, okay? I might not be very dependable, but if something's troubling you, I'd like to help you."

I want to know more about you, Monica. Those words that Saya had said to me were not a lie or a falsehood.

What she really thought had just come straight out of her mouth.

That's why...

"...You definitely won't tell anybody?" My mouth was moving before I realized. "I've never told this secret to anyone before. Not any acquaintances, not my parents, no one."

"I won't tell. Of course I won't." Saya nodded readily, her face brimming with trust.

I got the feeling that if it was Saya, she would accept me even if she knew the truth.

I felt like I wanted her to know the real me.

"I..."

And then...

On that day, I spilled my secret to her.

With just a few words, I revealed the secret that I had never told anyone, all these years.

"......"

In the twilight, Saya was quiet for a little while. Then, after a pause, she frowned as if wondering whether I might be joking. But she looked at my face and understood that it was no joke, and then finally, her cheeks flushed just a little.

"Is...that so...? That's...I'm a little...embarrassed..."

She didn't seem to find me repulsive. She simply believed my words and smiled.

I was happy.

"I like you." The words rushed out impatiently, and I smiled to try to cover my embarrassment. "And I like lots of things about you."

She was a hard worker. Diligent. Kind. She couldn't stand hurting others. She never lied. She didn't even tell little white lies. She just lived honestly in the moment, and I was dazzled by her.

I admired her so much, and I wished from the bottom of my heart I could live like she did.

So much so that I hoped—begged—to become the most important person in her world.

"Never change, okay, Saya?"

But I knew that there was someone else who already occupied the deepest reaches of her heart. I knew that there was no place for me there.

I had known everything from the time I was very small.

I had always been painfully aware.

O

Immediately after I had arrived in this place—in Emadestrin, a Town Where People Live, I had come face-to-face with Monica, and I was very surprised to see her.

The fact that the problems in her hometown hadn't been resolved yet had led me to believe that either Monica had left some time ago, or there was some other set of circumstances in play keeping her from addressing the problem.

When I had initially accepted the commission, concern for her well-being had been the biggest thing on my mind.

That's why I was surprised to see her.

I found it strange that Monica was still here in the city and hadn't cracked the case yet. It was unthinkable.

Because she knew everything.

Because the Monica that I knew could solve any problem.

Because several years earlier, she had told me a secret that she had never revealed to anyone else.

"I can read people's minds."

Because she had told me, and only me, the truth about herself.

When I'd arrived at Emadestrin and met up with Monica, I had immediately and intentionally closed my mind off.

I had forced myself to forget about the case and had gone to the main avenue that had absolutely nothing to do with it, where I had put on a show of wild, disordered reasoning.

At any rate, I had endeavored to think about nothing at all.

I had lied, too, and manipulated.

Even if it went against Monica's wishes, I couldn't allow her to read my thoughts.

"The reason why you've been dragging me around all day and night is that you think I might kill someone if you leave me alone…right?"

"……"

If Monica was still in this city but hadn't solved the murder cases, the truth was one of two options.

Either she was unable to catch the culprit for some reason, like, for example, they were threatening her, or were an acquaintance of hers, or something, or she herself was the killer. One of these had to be true.

But I had ruled out the former option. After a brief investigation, it became clear that there was way too little information about the killer.

It's almost as if they can see right through into the minds of all the townsfolk and can sneak around without anyone suspecting them.

It was strange that, despite the incidents happening for the past six months, not a single eyewitness could be found. The soldiers were supposed to be on patrol, and if they had spotted anyone suspicious, we certainly would have heard about it.

But I hadn't picked up on a single rumor.

This was not something that even a *hunter*-type murderer could have pulled off, let alone an *impulsive* type.

No one could have, except for Monica.

"…You've got some sort of problem, don't you? Some reason why you feel you have to kill…?"

I was positive she had a reason. I was certain that she had been driven into a corner, to the point where there was no way she could avoid doing it.

That was why I had begged her to let me help her.

"It's got nothing to do with you."

Unfortunately, my feelings didn't get through to her.

Monica was already gripping her wand, pointing it right at my face.

"If you leave me alone, I can let you go."

In other words, she meant...

"...So if I get in your way, you'll kill me?"

"You're quick on the uptake. That's a big help."

"......"

Since Monica could easily read anyone's mind, she was probably perfectly aware of what I was thinking at that moment.

She knew that I had absolutely no intention of backing down.

"...I see." Sorrow surfaced on her face. "...That's unfortunate."

Then she waved her wand.

Countless balls of fire appeared around her. Along with their radiance, I could feel their heat on my skin.

Before I could get my wand out, Monica flicked her wrist. That slight movement sent the fireballs flying toward me, one after another.

"*Tch—!*"

Just before they hit my face, I deflected the fireballs with water conjured from my own wand.

"Wait, please...Monica...! I—"

One by one, I extinguished the flames with orbs of water, countering her attack.

My mind was racing, wondering if there was anything I could say or do to get her to stop. I began to walk toward her, and to block my approach, Monica waved her wand again.

I had no intention of hurting her, and certainly no intention of killing her. So I wasn't able to use any highly lethal spells.

When Monica shot icicles at me, I shattered them. When she uprooted a streetlight and threw it at me, I changed its trajectory and dropped it onto the road.

I made almost no offensive moves myself.

The most I did was pull up garbage cans and flower beds from houses nearby and fling them at her in halfhearted attacks that were not even threatening.

But that didn't stop her.

"For someone who managed to become a witch, you use awfully unbecoming spells, don't you?"

"Is that what it looks like?"

"Yeah." Monica chuckled, then proceeded to smash every single object I had hurled at her into tiny pieces. "If you're not willing to cast real, lethal magic, you'll never stop me, Saya."

I tried to gather up all the scrap wood and bind her with it, but the moment the thought occurred to me, she had already set fire to the materials scattered all around us.

No matter what I attempted, she countered my spells.

"......"

But...

By no means was I at a disadvantage.

"...I didn't want to have to do something like this to you, Monica."

I gathered power into my fingertips and pointed my wand at her.

Since she could read her opponent's mind and was thus fully aware of the kinds of spells I was trying to cast, it was probably going to be difficult to stop her using superficial magic.

But that didn't mean that I couldn't stand up to her.

"I'm sorry," I said.

Then I fired a spell from my wand.

The first thing I fired off was a volley of fireballs, which she easily extinguished with balls of water, but immediately after the fire, a blast of wind pressed in on her. Of course, she had been able to anticipate that attack, too, and easily dodged it, but her reaction to the shower of icicles that loomed overhead was a little slow. Just then, there came the sound of an explosion from behind her, where the wind had destroyed the wall of a house, sending countless pieces of rubble to strike her in the back. Before her face could even distort with the pain, the next attack, an artless clump of raw magical energy, approached before her eyes, but she hit it with an identical clump of spell energy and they negated each other. In the momentary distraction that that provided, ivy broke through the red bricks that covered the ground and stretched upward until it seized Monica, but even this she calmly tore away. I launched the broken bricks directly at her face, but there couldn't have been much damage where they hit her, and all she did was look slightly displeased. But even so, I knew it would take a little bit of time before she noticed that the bricks had been a distraction just like the magical energy blast.

Because she released the tension from her arm, just for a moment, and when she extended it to make a counterattack, she was already no longer gripping her wand.

"……!"

That was the first time I had ever seen her look surprised.

In between hitting her gently in the face with ordinary bricks, I had managed to knock the wand out of her hand. Ivy wound around her feet again as she stood there, bewildered, after realizing that she had no wand, and this time I restrained her completely.

"…I'm sorry," I apologized again.

I had known from the beginning that she was able to read my mind. I had also known how to stop her if we ever got into a fight.

It was quite simple.

I just had to bombard her with so many spells that she couldn't keep up with all of them even if she could read my mind.

I had always known that I could stop her that way. I had been reluctant to do so only because I hadn't wanted to injure her.

"……"

I figured that she probably knew what I was thinking at that moment. Restrained, unable to move a muscle, she surrendered.

"I guess I was no match for a witch," she said with resignation, and smiled.

○

Word that Monica, the mage who was supposed to be working to protect the public peace, was actually the serial killer spread through the city immediately.

Everyone either shuddered with fear or shook with naked rage. This was only natural coming from the bereaved family members of her victims, but other related parties, as well as people who had, up until then, never spared a thought for the incidents, all attacked her without exception. It was not a surprising response to the news that the city's protector had actually been preying upon it.

The city was overflowing with animosity for Monica.

"Thank you so much for what you did, Lady Saya."

Even the government official who offered me a businesslike expression of thanks in a composed tone of voice probably felt the same.

"If you hadn't been here, she would probably still be going around killing people. I would truly like to express my gratitude…"

I'm sure that if I had been able to read minds like Monica, I wouldn't have been able to even look him squarely in the face.

"I was just doing my job," I said, shaking my head. "As for Monica… what will become of her now?"

"I suppose she'll receive punishment in accordance with the laws of our city."

"……"

"It goes without saying that the crimes she committed were of the utmost seriousness. She's a murderer. It might be appropriate to sentence her to capital punishment."

When a mage affiliated with the United Magic Association resolved a case and captured the culprit, one of two things happened.

Either the mage returned to the Association head office with the culprit in tow and a suitable punishment was meted out there, or the culprit received punishment in accordance with the laws of the country where the crime took place.

The former option was a special exemption that applied in countries where no laws had been established regarding mages, so as a general rule, the fate of the culprit was usually left to the local authorities. This was also beneficial for Association mages because it allowed them to finish up their cases quickly. However, considering the circumstances, I felt really, really reluctant to leave Monica in the hands of these people.

"…Will she be sentenced to death?"

I had discovered her true identity as a murderer.

I was even able to apprehend her.

But as for why she kept on killing people…when it came to that one point, she had stubbornly kept her mouth shut. I still had no idea why.

"Capital punishment in our city is not the death penalty." The official shook his head. Apparently, I had been mistaken. "We do not approve of any sort of killing here. Both suicide and homicide are, without exception, considered to be the most serious offenses. That goes for the death penalty as well. Issuing the death penalty for killing someone would seem to contradict our laws, don't you agree?"

"……"

But in that case…

"So what is the capital punishment here?"

The official answered me readily.

"Exile."

I walked through the city in a daze.

My business here was concluded. I had no other reason to remain in this city. I had finished everything I had come to do, so the logical thing to do would be to hurry up and fly my broom to the next place.

But for some reason, I couldn't leave.

Monica.

Ultimately, I still had no idea why she'd felt compelled to kill people, or what her goal was.

I wanted to see her just one more time.

That was why I was walking around the city in a daze.

"…You're Saya, right?"

And then…

Someone called out to me. When I turned around, a mage was standing there alone.

I had met her only once, but I remembered her.

Let's see, her name is…

"It's…Frauze…is that right?"

I was pretty sure she was the doctor who had performed the autopsies on the murder victims. I had met her only briefly when Monica and I had visited the hospital, so I wasn't entirely confident that I'd gotten her name right.

"Yes. I'm the coroner, Frauze." Apparently, I had gotten it right. "Do you have some time to spare right now?"

"……"

Her expression was cloudy.

I could tell that she was holding on to feelings that were completely different from those of most of the people living in the city.

"I've got something to tell you…about Monica."

"…What is it?"

She answered me briefly, "*We* knew the motive of the killer the whole time."

They knew yet stayed silent, she told me.

This was a weighty confession indeed.

●

Once I'd left the city, like my father had always wanted, I thought I would never go back again. I thought I would probably never see my father again.

That was why I answered with the same words every time, whenever Saya asked me whether I was planning to go back home after our training period was over.

"I have no intention of returning to my hometown."

Those words were not a lie.

Around the time our training came to an end, Saya, who had stayed with me even after learning that I could read people's minds, seemed to have forgotten our exchange not long after meeting, because she asked me in the same words as back then, "Once our training is over, are you going back home, Monica?"

I answered her honestly, "...It looks like I have no choice but to return."

Just before our training ended, a correspondence had reached me from Emadestrin, a Town Where People Live.

Written on the piece of paper was a long, businesslike message. But in summary, it basically said, *Your father has killed someone. He has received the punishment of exile. We need to discuss the issue of damages. Please return to the city promptly.*

That was all it said.

I had never expected to go back to my hometown again.

And yet in some part of my mind, the thought had occurred to me. The idea that a day like this might come sometime.

Awaiting me when I got back to the city were suspicious gazes for the only daughter of a criminal.

As soon as I got back, a city official told me just what kind of person my father had been. "Your father was a doctor, but he purposely administered dangerous drugs to his patients and ended their lives. He was a serial killer, I'm sorry to say. He must have been doing it the entire time that your family was living in this city; long enough that there were many, many victims. And as for the financial damages..."

The sum of money that was then presented to me was an amount that I could never possibly hope to pay off on my own.

The official told me that the city was going to use the money to ease the pain in the hearts of the families of the victims killed by my criminal father. And since my father had already been punished with exile, there was no other way than for me to pay it myself. They had already seized everything my father had saved up, and sold his house, but it wasn't nearly enough to satisfy his debt, which would now be forced upon me.

Then the official made a proposal.

"How about going to work for the city? Until the debt is repaid, you could devote yourself to the maintenance of public safety."

Since most of the local mages worked at the hospital, they had apparently been looking for someone to work for the city for a while.

What's more, I had a United Magic Association brooch hanging on my breast. Having me work for the city was probably ideal for them.

"Most of the people in this city know that you were on bad terms with your father. He abused you, and you got out when you couldn't stand it anymore, right? There are many who sympathize with your circumstances. I don't think anyone will object to your presence."

The official touched my shoulder as he spoke.

But I knew the truth.

I knew that my father had loved me more deeply than anyone else ever had.

I had never once been grateful for the ability to read people's minds.

As I walked around town, the animosity and discontent of other people echoed incessantly in my head. For example, two people exchanging words with smiles on their faces might secretly despise each other, or two lovers walking along hand in hand might not love each other at all. If I walked close enough, I could learn everything.

There was nothing that I didn't know.

Everything was perfectly clear to me, all the anger, pain, joy, and sadness that people were hiding deep in their hearts.

Of course, I also knew that my father had been killing people while working as a doctor.

But at the same time, I knew that he suffered more than anyone else in the city.

My father certainly had not been killing people for his twisted amusement. And he wasn't mad or cruel. He was neither an impulsive person, nor a hunter.

It was simply that he had no other choice but to end their lives.

The Lycoris Disease had ravaged the city for a long time, ever since I was a child, but no one had ever found a way to treat it. Once someone contracted the disease, the only thing the doctors could do was put the patient on magical life support, which was incredibly expensive.

These daunting sums, greater than any normal person could hope to pay, loomed over the patients' families. But in this city, euthanasia was as unforgivable as homicide or suicide. The doctors had to keep the patients on life support, which only drove their families further into debt. But euthanasia was forbidden, and so for the patient and their family, waiting for the end was nothing but endless suffering.

In order to save these people from their awful fates, my father had slipped certain lethal drugs into the patients' normal medications. He kept his actions a secret, bottling up the pain and refusing to confide in anyone as he thanklessly laid his patients to rest once and for all.

Every day, my father's spirit was worn away by his work. When he came home, he would lose himself in alcohol, and occasionally he even raised a hand to me. But I never once fell into despair.

Because I knew that my father's heart hurt worse than my cheek ever did.

Just as he had spent his life battling his own demons, I, too, stifled my own secrets. I lived by turning a deaf ear to people's grief.

When I was fifteen, my father said to me, "You're a magical genius.

It would be a waste for you to use your powers in a narrow-minded place like this."

But his true feelings were different.

My father knew. He knew that at some point his actions would come to light, and that the city would not be happy about it. My father was choosing a surface-level reason to drive me out of the city. But it wasn't because he hated me, or because I was a burden.

It was simply because he could see no point in me remaining here in this joyless city.

"Don't ever come back here."

Even the words that he said to me right before I left were a lie.

I knew what he really felt. I knew that my father wished he could be with me, that in his heart he hoped I would, in fact, return someday. But he was suppressing all these feelings.

So in the end…

When a letter arrived at the Association from Emadestrin, I resolved to return to the city.

The truth is that everyone thinks this city is strange.

They all have their doubts about the place, but they never say anything. They look away, choosing to believe that they themselves are the strange ones for having those doubts.

So they shut their mouths and put up with anything, no matter how unreasonable.

But I could hear everything.

My mind was filled with the anguished thoughts of the victims of Lycoris Disease, who still had no hope for recovery, and of the mages who had yet to discover a single successful treatment for the epidemic.

Someone has to tell them. Tell them that what they're doing is wrong.

Someone has to save them. Save these people from their endless suffering.

Someone has to become a martyr.

I know that.

And I know that revealing the truth does not always end in tragedy.

Even though I was the one who could hear the thoughts in people's minds, Saya was the one who had taught me that lesson, by not treating me any differently.

So even though I knew that my father hadn't wanted me to live the same kind of life he did, in the end, I walked down the same path.

○

"It's a famous story among the mages who work at the hospital."

Frauze told me the tale of Monica's father.

"Her father administered euthanasia to his patients, fully aware that it went against the laws of the city. He's been painted as someone who killed for pleasure, while ostensibly disposing of the dangerous drugs, but...at least among the mages who work at the hospital, Monica's father is something of a hero. That's because he accomplished something that no one else was able to do. Up to now, we have seen countless families destroyed by enormous medical expenses that drown them in debt. Your father saved people before it got to that point. We're under a strict gag order from the higher-ups in the city government, and this truth has never surfaced before, but..."

"......"

I answered her with silence, and she continued, "I can see most everything when I perform the autopsy. I've always known that all the victims to date were afflicted with Lycoris Disease."

"...Are you saying you kept quiet?"

There is nothing else that I can learn from this corpse. She had said something like that. I seemed to remember her also saying that she would do anything she could do to help.

"It's not just me." Raising her voice ever so slightly, Frauze stared back at me. "Most of the mages in this city are aware that every single murder victim was a Lycoris Disease patient."

"...In that case..."

Why didn't you tell me anything?

Frauze interrupted these words before they made it out of my mouth.

"We didn't want Monica to solve the case. Even though we knew that the government leaders had hung their hopes on her."

If Monica solved the case, the patients suffering from Lycoris Disease would be left without any relief again and would just have to suffer on in despair.

So the mages had decided to stay silent. That must have been why they found it so unpleasant when Monica came sniffing around trying to resolve the incidents.

But the person who had been saving the Lycoris Disease patients had been none other than Monica herself. Even when the people of the city called her incompetent for not being able to solve the case, and no matter how the mages at the hospital despised her, Monica had never revealed the secrets of her own heart to anyone. She had struggled on alone.

"Saya…"

By the time both of us knew all the details, Monica was already beyond our grasp.

"We've done something horrible to her…"

She fell down in a fit of unbearable remorse, and tears ran down her face.

"Recently, among the people I've met along my travels, there was someone a bit strange."

I recalled an earlier meeting I had with Elaina, a witch whom I hold in the highest regard. She told me one story from her travels.

A story about an amazing girl she'd met in a certain city.

"She could apparently see what was going to happen in the future, the next day, and the day after that. She could even see further, and she knew what was going to happen to the city, and how the people's lives would change, and things like that."

"Wow, that's a useful ability to have. If I had that kind of power, I'd probably use it to make lots of money."

I nodded noncommittally, and Elaina continued telling the story in an even tone of voice.

"But this girl never used her power to fulfill such selfish desires. Instead, she put her power to use by going around telling people's fortunes. She told one person, 'You'll have an accident tomorrow,' and another, 'Your partner is cheating on you,' and another, 'You will die in one month.' And all her predictions came true, just like she said. Though that was only to be expected, of course, since she could see the future."

"…So in short, she was going around harassing people?"

"Pretty much, yeah. That's what most people said about her."

"……"

"Why do you think she did it?" I had more questions. I wondered why on earth she would go around incurring people's anger like that.

There didn't seem to be any meaning behind it. Who on earth would choose for everyone to hate them, I'd wondered. Apparently, my inner thoughts were plain on my face, because Elaina answered my unspoken question.

"Well, you see, she wasn't just mindlessly getting involved in other people's affairs. Helping people avoid terrible fates meant dealing with their resentment. The girl knew that she couldn't ward off the unhappy futures that awaited them, but in order to keep their suffering to a minimum, she deliberately went around issuing prophecies that seemed like harassment."

Then Elaina said…

She told me…

"That girl…"

I wonder why I'm remembering that now?

And why is my chest tightening up like this, at what should be nothing more than a fun memory?

As I was running down the street, out of breath, I shook free of the memories of my conversation with Elaina that were flickering through my head. I was cursing myself for my own foolishness as I sprinted toward Monica.

The Monica that I knew was not the kind of person who would kill for pleasure. In fact, I was fairly certain she wasn't the sort of person who could do something like that lightly, even when compelled by absolute necessity.

Because she was much smarter than me, and a kind person.

"Excuse me!" I shouted as I ran.

I caught sight of the government official walking down the road ahead. He stopped, and without even waiting to catch my breath, I grabbed ahold of him.

The official's eyes opened wide with surprise at my sudden appearance. "Oh, Lady Saya…what's the matter?" He tilted his head quizzically.

I gripped him tighter and said, "Listen…! About Monica…! Where is she right now…!?"

I have to talk to her. I've got a duty to discover her true motives.

If what Frauze said is true… If Monica was actually driven to that path in order to save the people living in this city…

If that's what happened, then it would be completely wrong for the city to condemn her, wouldn't it?

Monica didn't do anything wrong, did she?

"Unfortunately, she is no longer in the city."

The official shook his head and tried to brush me off. "A short while ago, her exile was officially declared. She's probably already been escorted outside the city walls," he said readily and indifferently, then turned his eyes toward the borders of the city.

She's not here anymore…

That was simply the truth, but it set my heart pounding.

Elaina's words flashed through my mind.

"That girl understood the pain of others all too well."
I had a bad premonition.

•

In this city where killing people was not allowed, murderers were sentenced to exile. Apparently, the city didn't abide people who broke the law.
But no one knows.
They don't know what the punishment of exile really means.
"Stop."
I was bound with chains down to my fingertips, so that I couldn't even get my wand out. From behind my back, someone called out to me, and I did as they ordered.

There were two soldiers behind me. They were traveling with me, escorting me outside the city walls. They didn't see fit to exchange words with me, the criminal; they just hurled them at me, one-sided.

And since I could see what was in their hearts, and even knew the fate that awaited me, I didn't go out of my way to speak to them either.

"……"

Before me spread a bank of red flowers.

Their stalks stretched straight up out of the ground. Atop the stems were brilliant red blossoms, with petals spread out like fireworks. Here in the forest, with the blue sky stretching out overhead, the resurrection lilies were in full bloom all around us, completely blanketing the ground.

It looked like a lake of flowers, or perhaps like a sea of blood.

I figured that my father had probably also come here once, and the thought that I was standing in the same place *where my father had met the end of his life* filled me with complicated emotions.

Did you really think that monsters who killed other people would be permitted to go on with their lives outside the city walls? That just exiling them would be enough to make up for their crimes?

Of course not.

My father, and probably anyone else who committed a serious crime in Emadestrin, had surely met this same end. Punishing someone with exile was simply a means to an end in a country where all killing was prohibited.

I knew all this.

I even knew what my own final moments would be like.

"Do you have any last words?"

Behind my back, one of the soldiers hurled this emotionless question at me.

I looked back over my shoulder and shook my head.

"No."

"All right then."

Then the two soldiers started walking.

They trampled the resurrection lilies underfoot.

While pointing the tips of their spears at me.

My first victim was the homeless man.

His mind had told me that his body was afflicted with the illness. Knowing that he had contracted Lycoris Disease, he had abandoned his family, thrown away his social standing, and chosen the path of loneliness for himself. All this, he had told me without saying a word.

So I made him a proposal. I would put him to sleep with a spell and then end his life.

He had immediately accepted.

My second victim was the shop owner, for whom life was supposedly going smoothly. The discovery of Lycoris Disease during a checkup at the hospital had put him on the precipice of despair. I made my proposal. And he had immediately accepted.

My third victim was a very earnest student. She had become afflicted with Lycoris Disease and had chosen to kill herself. I'd stopped her and made her a promise to end her life painlessly instead.

Person after person had allowed me to bring their lives to an end with my own hands.

Those crimes had to be atoned for.

"Thank you."

Even though they had all worn smiles on their faces at the end, even though they had spoken words of gratitude to me as they died, these facts ultimately amounted to nothing.

"I'm sorry."

Even these words could be no comfort to all those people who had already taken their last breaths. Even the tears of remorse streaming down my face didn't change the fact that I had killed people.

I had to accept my punishment.

So I welcomed the blade that was thrust into me.

Before I realized it, the blue sky stretched out before my eyes.

The sounds of footsteps grew distant.

The two soldiers had not finished me off; they had just dealt me a fatal wound and then left. I was certain that this was what "exile" really meant.

Murderers were not allowed to die quickly, without suffering.

Suffering on and on, as much as possible.

The soldiers had left me only half dead.

With everyone else gone, now all alone, I extended a hand toward the sky, in the same position as all the people whose lives I'd ended.

And then...

"...Help me... Someone—Saya, help me..."

I let out the words that I had been keeping in my heart all along.

But with my hands bound by chains, I couldn't even beg for salvation.

○

In a place a short distance from Emadestrin, a Town Where People Live, there is a stretch of forest where the resurrection lilies bloom in great numbers.

And there was one particular place that was brimming with those blossoms, which Monica so loved.

I left the city and flew my broom around searching for her. I didn't know where she was, or if she had already long since gone off to another city, but when I found that spot, that bouquet of red blossoms, I was convinced that she must be there, too.

And sure enough, I spotted her there among the flowers.

"…Monica."

She was lying in the middle of a pool of crimson blossoms, staring up at the bright blue sky.

She was just lying there, her eyes open wide, as if absorbing the view.

The red flowers were wet with blood.

"…Saya."

She was still breathing. She turned her head heavily and looked at me with eyes wet with tears. "…You came."

I quickly cradled her in my arms.

If she's still breathing…

"Hang in there! I'll cast a spell right now!"

I can save her.

I pulled out my wand. If it was still possible to save her, then I thought I had a duty to do so, even if she was considered a criminal in her own city.

Because I was her friend.

"Don't…"

But she refused my help. She brushed aside my wand with hands bound and bloody.

"What are you—"

What are you doing? Do you want to die?

"You can't…," she answered resolutely. "No matter what you do, I don't have long…"

"…Huh?"

"Lycoris Disease."

She spoke those words shortly and concisely. Just two words. With only that, I knew the reason that she refused my help.

She said, "I don't have long."

The disease must have already eaten into her body. The same disease that had afflicted so many people living in Emadestrin was inside her, too.

"...But I want you to live. Even one second longer. So..."

So I picked up my wand, ready to try to cure her, even if she didn't want me to. With a hand now wet with her blood, I gripped my wand again. My fingers were trembling, and my aim was unsteady. My vision was also unusually blurry, and that's when I realized that I was sobbing.

Monica shook her head slowly at me.

Then she said, "Let me rest for now."

I replied, "...I can't. Please keep going. From now on, forever and ever..."

I wanted her to live forever. I wanted her to stay alive and keep on living. I begged her to stay by my side.

Through teary eyes, I watched her shake her head.

"...This is fine."

Then, stroking my cheek gently with fingers that were also bound by tiny chains, she said, "To be surrounded by the things I love in my final moments...there can be no greater happiness than this. It really is fine. Thank you."

With that, she smiled one last time.

I was about to say something more to her. I was about to cast a spell, but by the time I extended my hand, she was no longer with me.

She had fallen into a sleep from which she would never awaken.

Her face looked somewhat peaceful once she had entered her long rest.

I would never hear her voice again.

"...Say something..."

Yet still I spoke to her.

"...Say something, please..."

Even though she wasn't there anymore.

"Monica..."

Even though she was never coming back.

"Don't leave me..."

Even so, I kept on speaking to her, clasping tightly to the hands of the girl I adored.

○

The rest of the story I heard only secondhand, so I don't know how much of it is true.

I heard that not long after Monica's death, Emadestrin, a Town Where People Live, began to collapse. All the mages staged an insurrection and began euthanizing the people who had fallen ill, in imitation of Monica, and the disease spread out of control. These rumors and more made it to my ears, but unfortunately, I never got the chance to learn the real reason why the city fell to ruin.

That was because I never went anywhere near that place again.

"We've got a request from a country along the coast. You can read it on your way but be sure to look over their application form."

As always, the United Magic Association received requests from countries all over the world. And as always, convenient witches like me often got the troublesome jobs foisted upon us. That day, the request I looked over seemed like a real pain.

My teacher, Sheila, seemed to understand that, and she cursed the sender as she handed over the form. "Good grief, they always make such unreasonable requests..."

"...Understood."

After glancing quickly over the paper, I tucked it away in my pocket. As Sheila had said, I could read it through in more detail on my way.

I had a lot to do, and not a lot of time to do it, so I immediately turned on my heel and walked off.

That behavior must have seemed unusual for me, considering I ordinarily had nothing but complaints.

"...Are you okay?"

I heard Sheila call out to me from behind my back.

"……"

Unfortunately, I wasn't sure that I was okay.

But I didn't want to make my teacher worry…

"Yep."

…so I turned around and smiled.

"I'm fine."

Compared to the pain that Monica had held on to for so long, being busy with work was nothing.

So of course I was all right.

I left the United Magic Association branch office, and soon I left the city.

Small flowers bloomed beside the city gate.

Their stalks stretched straight up out of the ground. Atop the stems were brilliant red blossoms, with petals spread out like fireworks.

Resurrection lilies.

The ubiquitous flowers were poking out from the gaps in the cobblestones that covered the ground, swaying in the wind.

I'm sure that I'll remember every time I see those flowers.

I'll remember the girl who blossomed in solitude, more beautiful than anyone else.

CHAPTER 4

Cinderella

Lislette was a kindhearted young girl who lived in a castle town.

Her mother passed away when she was very young, leaving her father to raise her on his own. Lislette's father was kind and caring, and Lislette grew into a very good-natured young woman.

She and her father lived happily together.

Then her happy life suddenly came to an end.

Her father remarried.

His new wife seemed to dislike Lislette for some reason. She forced Lislette to do all the housework and constantly hounded her. Lislette's new stepmother also had two children from a previous marriage, and as one would expect of stepsisters, they, too, seemed to hate Lislette and always joined their mother in tormenting her.

All the chores were foisted onto Lislette.

"Clean my room, would you?" The elder of Lislette's stepsisters was a lazy girl who couldn't even pick up after herself, so she made a mess of her room and left it to Lislette to clean up.

"Y-yes...sister..." Lislette followed her instructions, wishing she could tell the lazy girl to do it herself.

Lislette's other stepsister was younger than her, but just like her older sister, she always pushed Lislette around.

"Hey. Take my clothes off for me. I want to get in the bath." For some reason, whenever the lazy younger sister wanted to get in the bath, she always made Lislette strip her down.

"Sh-shouldn't you...undress yourself...?" Lislette was hesitant to undress a girl so close to her in age.

"No! If you don't take my clothes off for me, I can't get in the bath! Wash my hair, too!" But the selfish younger sister refused and just continued to pester Lislette.

"Umm…"

Even though it was embarrassing, Lislette always took the other girl's clothes off for her.

However, even though she outwardly frowned at their treatment, Lislette thought her sisters were kind of cute, and she didn't especially hate cleaning their rooms or undressing them for baths.

What she hated the most was the job that her stepmother requested of her every day.

"Say, would you clean the hearth?"

Every morning as the sun came up, Lislette's stepmother would ask her to clean the hearth. Lislette had to sweep out the ash and cinders and prepare it so that it gave off warmth. Lislette had to do this job every day since the day she'd moved into her stepmother's house.

Lislette's beautiful golden hair would become absolutely filthy with ashes, just from cleaning the dirty hearth. She hated this chore most of all.

"Ugh…"

Even though she did it with a scowl on her face, Lislette never said anything about her stepmother's harassment. Every day she would clean the hearth, so her hair was always full of ashes. Being dirty all the time made her very sad, and eventually her eyes grew cloudy and her expressions darkened, and the only things that spilled from her lips were sighs.

Based on Lislette's outward appearance, she gained a nickname:

Cinderella.

As Lislette endured her stepfamily's harassment, she held on to one dream.

It would not be an exaggeration to say that her dream was what allowed her to endure the endless days of suffering.

"Eh-heh-heh-heh-heh…heh-heh…"

She was alone in the single small room that had been set aside for her. Shutting herself up in her room was one of Lislette's few pleasures in life. No one bothered her there. She would crouch down in the corner of this wonderfully lonely space, all alone, breathing heavily.

"Prince…my prince…eh-heh-heh…I wuv you…"

The brave girl who withstood constant bullying from her stepfamily would be replaced by an excited young woman, clutching a (secretly taken) photograph of the country's crown prince. In fact, there were (secretly taken) photos of the prince all over the walls. Anyone could see that this was the room of a stalker.

Lislette was head over heels in love with the prince.

She had never spoken to him, of course; they lived in two different worlds. In fact, Lislette had only ever managed to gaze at him from afar. The prince probably had no idea Lislette even existed.

But ever since she had laid eyes on the prince when she was younger, Lislette's head had been full of thoughts of him. To be frank, the harassment from her stepfamily and whatnot didn't cause Lislette much suffering at all. Just by gazing at one of her (secretly taken) photos of the prince, she could cleanse any patch of darkness that had taken root in her heart.

Well, who cares? It doesn't really matter, she thought. Lislette prided herself on her steely resolve.

"Eh-heh-heh… Wait for me, my prince…I'll come see you soon… eh-heh-heh…heh-heh…"

Recently, Lislette's mental fortitude had been tested even further.

Whether she was taking unreasonable, nonsensical requests like "Go and buy food for tonight's dinner! If you come back with the wrong ingredients, you'll go to bed without dinner!" or being told by her older stepsister to "remodel my room for me, Cinderella," or being asked, "Big sister Cinderella, dry my hair for me, will you?" she answered, "Gladly…eh-heh-heh…," and nodded with a broad smile on her face. That was how reckless her toughness had made her. Her willingness to put up with their awful treatment seemed to border on the verge of masochism.

Lislette believed that, very soon, her dearest wish would be granted.

"The grand ball…I can't wait…eh-heh-heh…"

The prince was to come of age that year, and he had too much wealth, power, and time on his hands. So sometime earlier, he'd decided that he ought to get married. It seemed a little crazy, but the prince had decided to go ahead and hold a grand ball anyway.

"Anyone and everyone is welcome to attend," the prince declared. "I'll have a wonderful feast prepared at the castle as well. And please remember that marriage is a *long-term* goal. I am absolutely not going to be choosing my bride during the ball, so don't worry about that. Please come and focus only on enjoying yourselves. Oh, but cute girls only, please!"

Many people were unhappy with this announcement, complaining that the event wasn't open to absolutely everyone—only cute girls. Ultimately, however, the prince used his considerable influence to silence any criticism of the ball, even going as far as to muzzle the newspapers and bribe certain key detractors. In that country, the people were weak in the face of money and power.

The ball was set to be held the following day.

Lislette was in especially high spirits. If she attended the grand ball, she would get to dance with the prince. None of her family's bullying could faze her.

"Eh-heh-heh…eh-heh-heh…"

And that day, as always, she spent every spare moment she had shut up in her room staring at the (secretly taken) photo of the prince, as if lapping it up with her eyes. Actually, she really did lick it, and smell it, and kiss it, and so on, pouring affection on it in every conceivable way. The photo was already messy with drool, but even so, Lislette's excitement knew no bounds.

Her spirit was already somewhere else.

Since the day the ball had been announced, Lislette's mind had

©Azure

been full of wild fancies concerning her sweet, sweet married life with her future husband, the prince.

"……"

Lislette's stepfamily secretly watched her reverie.

The older stepsister turned pale. "Cinderella…"

The younger stepsister shed a tear. "Big sister…"

Their mother sighed. "…This is awful."

Even a charitable observer would have had trouble believing the extent of Lislette's unnatural obsession.

Perhaps she had retreated into fantasy as a natural consequence of her stepfamily's daily abuse.

O

The entire castle town was getting ready for the grand ball that was happening the following day. From the moment we arrived, we already felt like we were ready to turn and flee.

The low buildings of the town stood side by side, as if lined up to wait upon the royal palace that towered over them. Everywhere throughout the town, flyers were posted up, advertising the grand ball that was going to be held at the palace. They read: THE CROWN PRINCE IS HOSTING A BALL. GIRLS ATTEND FOR FREE (※ OFFER LIMITED TO CUTE GIRLS ONLY). The prince's flagrantly ulterior motives were plain for anyone to see.

I had only just arrived in the city. I'd scarcely made it through the gate, found the nearest hotel, and set down my luggage. I had no idea what the place was usually like, but I was pretty sure it didn't look like this all the time.

"Oh-hoh-hoh… How do I look? This is what I'm wearing to the royal ball tomorrow!" a girl wearing a luxurious dress boasted to her friend.

"…Eh-heh-heh… As long as I've got my love potion, the prince doesn't stand a chance…" Another girl was going shopping, grinning to herself.

"Say, did you know? The prince apparently likes girls with pretty feet."

"I heard. He seems to especially like girls in high heels."

"Why heels?"

"Maybe he likes getting stepped on?"

"Oh, prince…"

Two girls were choosing high heels in a shoe store, whispering rumors to each other.

"Seems like my granddaughter is going to the ball."

"Oh? Mine too."

"Ha-ha-ha! I bet mine is going to be the one he picks."

"No, no, my granddaughter will be the one."

"No way."

"No way, no way."

Two old men were conversing restlessly.

In this way, the whole town had become obsessed with the grand ball.

All the girls seemingly waiting for their chance to live a dreamy, glamorous life in the castle that loomed on high must have thought that this ball was their chance to strike it rich.

"Elaina…" As I was gazing vacantly out over the town, Miss Fran, who was standing beside me, poked my shoulder with her fingertip. "Elaina, what are you going to do?"

What will I do?

"…Don't tell me you think that I'm going to go to the royal ball?"

"No, not that." Miss Fran shook her head. "Actually, I've got something I have to do here, so we've got to go our separate ways for a little while."

"Huh? Something you have to do?" I was quite intrigued by her ambiguous way of saying it. "Don't tell me *you're* going to the ball?"

"I've been entrusted with a special job. I have no interest in marrying into wealth."

"Uh-huh."

Well, there's no reason for us to to stick together twenty-four-seven, so I don't have any cause to object.

Nonetheless, it did make me feel quite lonely that she hadn't told me why on earth she needed to be alone.

"It's fine, I understand."

For the time being, I nodded at her.

"…By the way, what's the job?" I asked, though I didn't expect that she would tell me.

"It's a secret."

Sure enough, Miss Fran chuckled and put her index finger to her lips.

Then she said, "I think I'll be back this evening, so let's have dinner together then. My treat."

As she spoke, she turned her back on me and started walking off.

"……"

I waved good-bye to my teacher.

I waved at Miss Fran, who was, in all probability, headed off with her eye on the prince.

"……"

She's really awful at keeping secrets…

And so the curtain went up on my solo act.

As I wandered around the expansive city, I realized that even though I had spent most of my journey alone, I now missed having someone beside me. I felt bored. Probably because my conversation partner had suddenly disappeared.

That said, even though I was used to traveling on my own, it wasn't like I wanted to be alone forever. I'd experienced this unpleasant sort of loneliness and boredom before.

Usually when this happened, I changed my broom into human form so that she could help me pass the time. But for some reason, I suspected that if I changed her into her human form at that moment,

she would just complain about it and make fun of me for being so lonely in my teacher's absence.
I've got to stop relying on my broom for companionship.
"This is awful, big sister... If we don't do something, our Cinderella will..."
"Yes...in times like these, I wish we had a mage to help us..."
......
Of course, I was just a humble traveler. Even though I had some time to spare, I wasn't necessarily thinking about meddling in someone else's troubles or helping anyone in need.

And so, even when I noticed the two girls crying softly by the side of the road, my response was simply to walk on by without stopping.

"This is awful, big sister... If we don't do something, our Cinderella will..."
"Yes...in times like these, I wish we had a mage to help us..."
......
I felt that I had heard the exact same two lines mere moments ago, but as before, I ignored everything. *I'm pretty sure I passed them by, so how did I hear the same words again? An echo, maybe?*

"This is awful, big sister... If we don't do something, our Cinderella will..."
"Yes...in times like these, I wish we had a mage to help us..."
......
When I heard the same words for the third time, I finally turned around.

Even I wasn't oblivious enough to miss the fact that someone was trying to get my attention. Apparently the two girls had zeroed in on me as I passed them by, and then they began following me.

The two of them were standing directly behind me, and they whispered to each other as they looked over at me intently, as if they were sizing me up or something.

"Big sister...this girl..."

"She seems useful, doesn't she? …She's very cute, too…"

I narrowed my eyes at them and asked, "Do you have some business with me?"

"Oh, no! It's nothing as serious as all that!" The older sister shook her head.

"If you don't have any business, then why were you following me?" I demanded.

That's pretty creepy, isn't it?

"We just thought you were really pretty, and kind of followed you," said the younger sister, without seeming the least bit ashamed.

"I see."

If it's because I'm pretty, then it can't be helped, I suppose.

"And so we have a favor to ask you, since you're so pretty," the older sister said, and quickly bowed her head. She must have completely forgotten what she'd said just a moment earlier.

So you really do have business with me, and that's why you were stalking me, is that right? Well, I could more or less figure that much out already.

"…Well, I'll listen to what you have to say, at least." I nodded. "Unfortunately, I don't have any time to spare, so I can't promise that I'll be able to help you."

That's a lie, though. I've got nothing else to do.

"Oh! Really?" But the older sister seemed to take my words to mean that I would agree to their request, because her face lit up as she launched into the story.

"The truth is…"

"……"

My goodness.

I didn't really understand her story, and it was pretty strange, but I did know one thing for certain. It was intriguing.

●

"...I'm terribly sorry. Could you possibly explain it again from the beginning?"

Oh, I wonder what Elaina is doing right now? If I know her, she's probably sightseeing, or maybe just killing time. But then, she also has a tendency to get caught up in complicated situations, usually at the worst possible moment.

So maybe right now, Elaina's making faces as some stranger tells her their story... Maybe she's overheard some interesting conversation and is sticking her nose in someone else's business... I'm very worried, as her teacher...

These thoughts and more were running around in my head.

The details of my commission, which the prince had conveyed with exaggerated gestures from atop his throne, had not stuck in my head at all. Just like my butterflies, they had all fluttered away.

"Huh...? I have to tell you again, from the beginning...? It's not exactly the kind of thing you repeat over and over...this is a top secret job."

The prince let out a sigh.

He had glossy blond hair, which he pushed back from his face with a strangely charming gesture. He sighed. "Well...I suppose it can't be helped..."

Then, with an air of importance, he told me, "To give you a rough idea, I want you, Lady Witch, to help me find my future wife! Basically, I want you to take on the role of my advisor!" He was saying everything awfully loudly, considering this mission was supposed to be top secret.

"......"

Ah, indeed, I see. So that's what this is about. I remember now.

It was such a stupid—no, such a distasteful *request, considering his status, that it flew right out of my head. How unfortunate.*

According to the paperwork I'd been given, the prince apparently had too much time on his hands. Lately, he had become consumed by a singular desire—his wish to find a bride. Which had led him to the notion of holding a royal ball, so that he could meet someone worthy of his courtship.

In short, he just wanted to get married. That was the whole point of the discussion.

"Yes, yes, a marriage partner, is it? In that case, how about holding some interviews?" I started with a commonsense suggestion.

"*Tch!*"

Apparently common sense just wouldn't do for his royal highness.

"I believe in the supremacy of free love… I'm opposed to the very idea of holding marriage interviews. Besides, if someone of my station were to hold interviews, the only girls who would show up would be the ones lured by the promise of wealth."

"Well then, how about holding the interviews but masking your status?"

"Hold on now," the prince huffed in frustration. "If you strip me of my status, I've got nothing left to offer…" Then he let out a long sigh.

What a miserable young man…

"Wait right there, Madam Witch!" Just then, an old man marched in from the throne room. "When did you hire an advisor?! Gramps does not approve!"

Apparently, the old man who called himself "Gramps" had stealthily overheard the prince's top secret request.

"Quiet, Gramps!" the prince answered, raising his voice deliberately. "I am the prince of the whole country! I'll use any method I like in order to marry the best girl I can find!"

Despite all his prestige, the prince's words revealed him to be little more than an ordinary jerk. This put me in something of a bind.

I sighed, "Um…do you really want to get married that badly…?"

"Yes, I do. Of course I do." The prince spoke confidently from start to finish. "By the way, Lady Witch, can you brew a love potion? I'm just curious, of course."

I wish he wouldn't be so confident even about his vulgar thoughts…

"You mustn't do that, prince! Gramps will not allow you to use a love potion!" Gramps tried to hold the reckless prince in check. "…But, ah, Lady Witch…is it even possible to make one…?'

Oh, Gramps…

Wait, more importantly…

"It seems to me that using a love potion would be in direct opposition to the idea of free love…"

"Free in the sense of living inside a cage."

I don't think you can call that freedom anymore…

At any rate, the conversation had gotten rather off track, but to put it simply, the reason that the prince had summoned me there was…

"So would it be fair to say that you want my help seducing a girl at the royal ball?"

The request that had brought me all the way out to this castle had said that it was an important matter that required my talents. But upon arriving, all that had happened was that I'd been subjected to the crude, adolescent whining of a spoiled prince caught at the height of puberty, whose mind was dominated by lust. It made me want to cry.

If this is what he wants from me, it would be a much better use of my time to go sightseeing around town with Elaina…

"No! What part of my story were you listening to?!" The prince slammed his fist against his throne, revealing his anger.

What's this? Could it be that what he has said so far was just nonsense, nothing more than idle talk? Of course, it would be improper for an actual prince to go out of his way to summon a witch just because he wanted her to help him put on a grand ball. Someone who did that would be less of a prince and more of an ordinary jerk, after all.

"I want to find a girl who will step on me in high heels. Not just a normal wife. Please make sure you understand me clearly."

It turned out the prince was a pervert.

"This won't do, Your Highness!" the old man who called himself Gramps interjected. "That's my fantasy!"

Oh, Gramps…

"If possible, I want a girl to step on me while looking at me with cold eyes, like I'm a piece of garbage."

"I hear that."

Oh, prince…

I have to wonder how this country has managed to hold itself together this long…

"So anyway, I'm counting on you, Madam Witch."

"……"

I'm not sure how to respond to that.

"And if I don't help you…would that be bad…?" I muttered.

"Ha-ha-ha!" The prince laughed cheerfully. "No, I wouldn't mind if you refused my request. But if you did, you would probably find yourself unable to leave the country."

"……"

Does that mean I don't have the right to refuse…?

It turns out the prince is an incredible lowlife.

○

"The prince who rules the country is a creep…? Seriously?"

The two sisters who approached me on the street told me that their stepsister, Lislette, who had started living with them the previous year, was deeply in love with the prince. They wanted me to do something about it.

I figured that they were going to ask me to help dissuade a girl who had forgotten her station and fallen in love with the prince, or ask me to explain to her that she wouldn't be able to win the prince's heart even if she did go to the ball, or deal with the situation in some clever way using my magic powers. That was the sort of thing I was expecting them to ask. But reality turned out to be stranger than fiction.

The girls invited me to their house, and the truth that they shared with me was completely different than anything I'd expected.

"The truth is, a long time ago, we worked as maids in the royal palace. Back then, we cleaned the prince's chambers, and..." The older sister broke down sobbing.

The younger sister placed her hand on her sister's shoulder and said, "...There were a lot of strange magazines stuffed under his bed..."

Well now, that doesn't seem like something to cry over.

"...Well, if he's a young man, of a certain age, it's not unusual that he would take an interest in...such things," I said.

But the older sister just kept crying. "We wouldn't be so upset if they were ordinary dirty magazines! But we never imagined...we never imagined the prince would be such a degenerate..."

Apparently, there had been a time when the two sisters had actually adored the prince, just like Lislette, but they said that once they'd discovered what was under the prince's bed, any feelings they'd had for him had completely evaporated. They told me that now they could only see him as a beast in princely clothing.

I was somewhat morbidly curious to learn exactly what kind of magazines they'd found, but I decided to set that feeling aside and talk about the job instead.

"So you want me to work with you to open Lislette's eyes, now that she's fallen for the prince?" I asked.

The younger sister nodded in the affirmative. "We will never hand over our dear, darling sister Cinderella to that pervert! Help us, Miss Witch!"

"Can't the two of you persuade her on your own?"

Is this actually such a serious problem that you need to involve a full-fledged witch? I'm very doubtful.

"...At first, we did try to persuade her. We told her everything, leaving nothing out, and explained what a creep he is...," the older sister said, casting her eyes downward.

That had taken place right after the girls' mother had married Lislette's father.

"Oh? So you like the prince, Lislette...?"

Just after they had become family, Lislette had invited her new stepsister into her room, and the older girl had recoiled at what she saw there.

"Hm? How could you tell, big sister?"

She could tell because one wall was plastered with (secretly taken) photos of the prince.

What a wretched situation that must have been. The pure, beautiful young girl had a crush on the prince, who seemed like a fairly good person on the outside but was rotten on the inside. Something had to be done.

The older sister had explained kindly, "Lislette, listen..."

Then she had told Lislette about what she had seen when her family was in the employ of the prince. She'd explained that he was a pervert with a bizarre obsession.

She had figured that once Lislette heard about the prince's true nature, she would probably give up on him, too.

However...

"How cruel! You two just want to get in the way of our romance! I hate you so much!"

Lislette ended up turning on her older stepsister.

The older girl had been smitten with Lislette's cute appearance ever since she first laid eyes on her, and the rejection hurt her so deeply that she spent three days laid up in bed.

After that, the older stepsister tried every method she could think of to open Lislette's eyes to the truth. She took every opportunity to mention the prince's awful reputation. The younger sister and stepmother also did their part to persuade Lislette, to open her eyes to the truth after she had fallen for the good-for-nothing prince.

But she wouldn't listen to them.

So instead they started forcing extra work on her, practically harassing her every day, though it hurt them to do so. They hoped she would be too busy to think about the prince.

And that was apparently the whole story.

I see, I see.
"So it backfired?"
"I guess it backfired." The older sister tilted her head thoughtfully. "She's so infatuated with the prince that it's almost like she's been afflicted with some strange madness. The more we try to interfere, the hotter her passion burns." The girl was obviously in very low spirits. "...So everything that we've done so far was for nothing?"

"Well," I mused, "from what I've heard of the present situation..."

If Cinderella wanted to attend the grand ball, then they had obviously not cured her of her obsession with the prince. Actually, the sisters had probably stoked the fires instead.

"Anyway! Lady Witch! Please! We cannot possibly hand Lislette over to the prince! Help us!" the older sister moaned as she clung to me.

"I'm begging you, please!" the younger sister groaned. "If big sister Cinderella goes away, who will wash my hair!?"

Couldn't you wash it yourself...?

"......"

I thought for a moment.

I'm not really busy, and I don't mind helping them, but...

"So basically, you'll be happy so long as the prince doesn't fall for her at the ball? Is that really something that you have to worry about?"

If I were to make a succinct comparison, it was like someone resentfully declaring, "A person I hate bought a lottery ticket! If I don't do something, he's gonna strike it rich! I can't allow it!" Honestly, I was bewildered that they had approached me with this issue, wondering what I could possibly do.

But the older sister grew very, very angry at my words.

"What a horrible thing to say! If she attends the ball, there will be chaos! She's too cute!"

What are you talking about? I don't understand what you mean.

It didn't seem like I could say that out loud, so I just smiled ambiguously. "Uh-huh..."

"Big sister Cinderella is the cutest girl ever, so of course the prince will fall for her. Are you stupid?" Then I received a scathing judgment from the younger sister as well.

I just stared off into the distance. "Oh, sure...of course..."

"Anyway, Miss Witch, please get her to give up on the prince immediately," the older sister said decisively.

"......"

Wait, hang on, actually...

"Couldn't you just keep her from going to the ball?"

It seemed like common sense to me.

However, it was pretty clear that these girls were way past the point of common sense, because of that deviant prince.

"Don't say stupid things!" they said.

"If possible, we want to see Cinderella in her ball gown!"

"......"

Perhaps those magazines that were under the prince's bed have something in them that drives you crazy if you read them?

Be that as it may, a job was a job, so there was no point in whining about it. As much as I wanted to ditch them at some point on the way to their home, I was a little worried about what the two crazy sisters would do if I'd tried.

At that point, I decided to prepare myself for the worst.

"That's our sweet Cinderella."

The sisters and I were stealthily peeking into the kitchen from a hidden spot. In our line of sight was a girl with beautiful golden hair that was filthy with ashes, diligently cleaning the hearth.

Directly behind her was a woman who appeared to be the stepmother, standing there motionlessly, staring at the girl.

"...*Hff, hff...*"

But the woman seemed awfully distressed. I wondered what on earth was the matter.

"Um, does your mother have some sort of chronic disease or something?"

The sisters shook their heads decisively.

"No, she's not sick," said the older sister.

So then, what is it?

"She's fascinated watching Cinderella doing her work."

I see—so she is sick.

"Anyway, please help us, Miss Witch. Make Cinderella happy somehow…!"

"……"

I have a feeling she'll never be happy, so long as she's in this house…
Well, whatever.
Let's get on with the job.

"Hello."

I popped out unexpectedly, right behind the two of them.

"Oh! And you are?"

The stepmother turned around abruptly. There was no hint of the heavy breathing I'd heard from her a moment before. Apparently, she only got excited when she was looking at Cinderella, or whatever it was they had called the girl.

"I'm a friend of your daughters."

"……" After making deliberate eye contact with the two sisters, who were both right behind me, the stepmother said to me, "Hello there, Miss Witch. What can I do for you?"

She smiled brightly at me. If I hadn't seen her acting strangely just a moment before, she would have seemed like an ordinary mother.

"Would it be all right for me to speak with Lislette for a moment?" I tilted my head questioningly.

The stepmother nodded, "Yes, of course. She is one of my precious daughters, so make good friends with her, all right?"

Then she hurriedly joined the two sisters in their hiding spot.

"She's quite cute, isn't she?"

"She is. But not as cute as my Cinderella."

"Yeah. Big sister Cinderella belongs to me, though."

"......"

I can hear everything you're saying...

I took a step forward to escape the disturbing atmosphere that was developing behind me. Lislette had been cleaning the hearth the whole time, and I tapped her on the shoulder.

"Hello."

"Eee!" She jumped with surprise just like a small animal and turned around. "...Ah, h-hi..."

She seemed terrified.

"Cinderella is so cute!"

"Big sister Cinderella is adorable!"

"*Hff...hff...*"

I could hear some weird voices and heavy breathing behind me, but I did my very best to ignore them.

All this weirdness might rub off on me if I stick around too long...

I decided to finish up my job right away.

"Are you in love with the prince?"

"......!" As soon as I asked, she gave me a reaction that was very, very easy to understand. "H-how did you...?! Where did you hear that?! A-and from whom?!"

Lislette was yanking on my skirt.

"Hey now..." I slapped at her grasping hands. *What is this girl doing?* I wondered. "No, I can tell just by looking at you..."

"You can tell by looking...? What do you mean by that? Can witches tell what kind of person someone is just by looking at them?"

"Uh...yeah. So that's enough of that." I kept slapping at her hands. "By the way, that means that I can also tell what kind of person the prince is."

"......!"

Upon hearing that, she finally let go of me. Straightening myself up, I looked down at Miss Cinderella.

"Do you want to know?"

"............!" She nodded with stiff movements, like a broken doll.

In that case, allow me to enlighten you.

"He's human garbage."

"Human garbage..."

"And a real beast."

"A beast..."

"What's more, he has a very peculiar fetish."

"A peculiar fetish...?"

"Apparently he likes to be stepped on by high heels."

"Likes to be stepped on by high heels..."

I added my own embellishments midway through. But that really was the kind of person the prince was.

Apparently Lislette had written off her sisters' criticism of the prince as a form of bullying. I wondered what would happen if she heard the same thing from an outside source.

I expected it would make something of an impression on her.

"...I see, yes..."

Lislette hung her head sadly.

Apparently, the plan had been a success. I turned back around and walked over to the sisters and their mother, who had been watching us.

"And with that, I believe my work is done here."

I didn't even have to use magic! I wore a triumphant expression.

But...

"......" The older sister was looking past me. "It's not over just because some stranger told her that..."

She was looking at Lislette.

"Heh-heh-heh..."

For some reason, Lislette was laughing.

"He's a prince, but he's scum? That's the best... I'm in love..."

For some reason, she was saying things I couldn't comprehend.

I see—it seems like she's already reached the point where no matter what anyone says, she can't take it as anything but validation for her feelings.

I know love is blind, *but this is a little extreme…*

"……" I looked back at the sisters. "She seems like she'll get along quite well with the prince, doesn't she?"

"That's the problem!" The older sister let out a sigh.

Apparently Lislette's fondness for the prince far exceeded anything I'd anticipated, and no matter what happened, her passion for him never cooled.

After my initial attempt, I started to take things more seriously. I told Lislette all about the prince's bad reputation, but…

Even when, for example, I told her a lie, like: "Did you know? Apparently, the prince is an unrepentant philanderer."

"He's so attractive…that can't be helped…"

She quickly accepted it, showing how tolerant she was.

When I told her: "Apparently the prince has some real funky body odor."

She replied: "Oh, how exquisite…"

For some reason, she swooned, and her heart began racing even faster.

I even tried a roundabout way to shut her down, saying: "Apparently the prince has someone he likes already."

"Well, if *I* can get him in bed first…"

Lislette had other, terrible ideas.

In short…

"This has already gotten way out of hand, hasn't it?" I grumbled.

"Do you see now? Even if we're as direct as can be, our efforts have absolutely no effect…" The oldest sister let out a sigh, at her wit's end.

"If we don't do something, an awful man will take our big sister Cinderella away…," the younger sister mourned.

Troublingly, the sisters seemed to have nothing in their heads except thoughts of Lislette.

Despite the fact that all my attempts had been in vain, they begged with tears in their eyes, "Please, Miss Witch! Please do something!"

I was at a loss.

If I'm being completely honest, I wanted nothing more than to get out of there. But I was in too deep already. I couldn't just abandon ship.

But if nothing we tried worked, then what else could I do...?

"So it's impossible after all... A task too great, even for a witch..." Behind the grumbling sisters, the stepmother let out a sigh. "Looks like we have no choice but to use our last resort..."

Then the stepmother fixed her gaze on me.

"......?"

What?

I tilted my head in confusion, and she continued, "The fact is, we have a much easier way to protect our dear Cinderella from the evil clutches of the prince."

Oh-hoh. In that case, wouldn't it have been better for you to use that method to begin with?

The sisters looked at each other.

"Mother...you're planning to do *that*?" The older sister gazed at her mother with fear on her face.

By the way, what is that?

"You intend to offer up a living sacrifice, don't you...?" The younger sister looked up at her mother, her eyes filling with tears.

By the way, what's a living sacrifice?

"There's no helping it... This is the only way we have left to protect our Cinderella..."

Then the stepmother stood up.

"......"

By the way, why is she staring right at me?

●

"I'm exhausted..."

I can only assume that people lose all sense of reason after they fall in love. After listening for some time to the requests of the prince, who, despite being of age, was still right in the midst of puberty, I returned to my hotel.

After being subjected at length to his delusions, he finally made his proposal. "So the plan is that I'm going to invite lots of girls to the grand ball tomorrow, and you are going to slip in and dose them all with a love potion."

"Wait, but I can't make anything like a love potion…"

"Ha-ha-ha! Surely you don't expect me to believe that a witch wouldn't know how to make a simple love potion! You mustn't lie, now."

"No, really, that's not something I can do."

"Anyway, I'm counting on you for tomorrow."

"……"

The prince had apparently summoned me here so that I could make him a love potion, but he had completely overestimated me. Since I knew very little about romance, I had never had the opportunity to make such a potion, or to try one out, so I truly couldn't fulfill the prince's request.

Though, as far as I could see from the state of the town, countless numbers of girls wanted to attend the prince's ball, so I honestly doubted there would be any need for me to make a love potion in the first place.

Surely the prince would be satisfied if I picked one of the girls attending the ball—one of the girls who was really, really infatuated with the prince—and then presented her to him.

"……"

But finding a girl who was in love with the prince…would be an arduous task.

To begin with, love is something that is secreted away inside a person's heart, is it not? An outsider cannot tell whether someone is in love with someone else.

It's possible that someone might be in love, but still bewildered by their own feelings, and letting out strangely anxious sighs as they struggle with their woes, but fundamentally, that's not something that's apparent from the outside.

"...Sigh."

If, for example, someone suddenly starts acting very differently—like Elaina, for example, who just now let out a sigh as she was staring out the window—then maybe that person might be in love, but...

If that person was an old friend, I'd think that I would notice even the smallest signals, but with a bunch of strangers, there's no way that I'll be able to tell which girls have really fallen in love with the prince.

"Oh, Elaina. What's the matter? Is something troubling you?" I asked.

Finally, Elaina turned around to face me. "Ah...Miss Fran. You came back. Welcome back."

"......"

For instance, when people fall in love, they get tunnel vision and start ignoring everything else around them. Why, if I had to describe it, I'd say they act just like Elaina is acting now, but...huh? No, no...what?

"...What's the matter, Elaina?"

Of course, people who are in love aren't quick to open up about their drama.

"...Oh, nothing."

"......"

Oh my.

And despite not opening up, they let out lots of troubled sighs.

"...Hahhh."

Just like that.

"......"

Oh my.

What on earth happened in the short time we were apart?

"Miss Fran...can you make love potions and stuff?"

"??????????"

Oooooohhh?

Seriously, what happened...?

"E-Elaina...?"

What on earth could have happened to Elaina? We were only apart for half a day! I don't think this could be it; it's a ten-thousand-to-one chance, but maybe she's fallen hard for some boy she met around town? No, no, this is Elaina we're talking about. I doubt something like that would ever happen. I'd like to think it could, but... Anyway, the Elaina before my eyes is the very picture of a girl in love. I have no idea what I should do... Well, I suppose I can't help being perplexed over what to say to her...

It took all my effort to ask her timidly, "Um...? Did something happen while I was gone...?"

"......"

After a long and dreadful silence, Elaina answered briefly, "...No, nothing really."

"......"

But if she's fallen in love, who on earth could be the object of her affection?

"Come to think of it, you went to see the prince today, didn't you, Miss Fran?"

"Huh? Uh...yes, I did..."

"What kind of person is he?"

"...!"

Has she fallen for the prince...? Seriously...?

"Elaina..."

I was overwhelmed by the discovery that my favorite pupil, whose growth I'd watched over so carefully all these years, had, in a mere half day, given her heart to a man whom I could only describe as a total jerk. I started sobbing.

How could such a sad reality actually come to pass...?

"Huh...? Miss Fran? Why are you crying...? It's creepy..."

I suppose it goes without saying that I fell asleep that night full of regret. If I had known that something like that would happen, I would have ignored the commission from the prince and spent the day sightseeing with Elaina.

○

I had been feeling awful all morning.

"It suits you perfectly, Madam Witch! If you wear this, the prince won't stand a chance!"

Lislette's stepmother and her daughters squealed in unison when they saw me in the dress. "So cute!"

One of them also added something unnecessary. "I feel like she doesn't quite fill out the bust, but it'll be fine!" I was seized by the impulse to tear the dress off, but I let out one dismal sigh instead.

How on earth had I wound up in such a situation? It was all part of the horrendous plan that the stepmother had laid out the day before.

"Wouldn't it be nice if the witch could attend the ball and win the prince's heart instead?"

Wait just a minute, what's nice about that?

I was completely bewildered, but she continued, "We need you to win over the prince real quick, pretend you're going to marry him, and then dump his ass. If you do that, don't you think he'll learn that he can't find happiness choosing a girl based solely on her looks?"

What on earth are you talking about, with that expression on your face like you hit upon some great idea? And what do you mean by "solely on her looks"?

Agreeing with their mother, the two sisters chirped in unison, "This way no one will end up unhappy!"

But I'm already unhappy…

"So once the marriage is in the bag, you can just run away!" said the younger sister. "And while you're running, you might consider 'borrowing' some valuables." She whispered this devilish suggestion.

Exactly what do these two girls think of me?!

"There is no way I would stoop to stealing a few trinkets from the palace!"

Don't underestimate me, girls. I am a witch, you know!

"…If I'm robbing the place, I'm taking everything."

To be honest, even despite everything that had happened, I still couldn't help myself. I was starting to get excited about the plan. It was almost like the sickness of the toxic family had rubbed off on me.

But once I got back to the hotel, the more I thought it over, the trouble of having to enter a temporary sham engagement with the prince started to overshadow the appeal of the treasure in the palace. I found myself sighing frequently.

And so, even though I had allowed the stepmother and her daughters to put me in a dress for the day, I wasn't taking any pleasure in it. I ended up just grumbling and complaining the whole time.

"What a pain…"

"Now, now, don't say that." The stepmother clapped a hand down on my shoulder. "Leave Cinderella up to us. We'll load her down with an absurd amount of chores so that she can't even go to the ball. That should buy you plenty of time. And while we're doing that, you'll seduce the prince."

"…*Sigh*."

I answered with another sigh.

At any rate…

That's how I ended up attending the royal ball.

●

It was evening. The sun was just beginning to drop below the horizon.

The palace gates were thrown open and crowds of young ladies, each clad in a splendid dress, rushed in all at once. The parade of girls blinded by the promise of money reminded me of a herd of wild animals repeating some great migration in search of new pastures.

I wonder if there really is a cute girl in that crowd who will suit the prince's tastes? They all look the same to me.

"All right, Miss Witch, if there are any girls here who I might like, it's up to you to set them up with me. I want to pretend I'm approaching them by chance in all cases. If we let slip how starved for love I am, they'll only be disillusioned, you see. I'm counting on you."

"……"

Well, there's not much point in hiding your desperation, now that the ball is already underway, is there...?

The girls kept assembling one after another in the hall. Naturally, since the prince was adamant that the event was an actual ball, there had to be other boys as well. I could see them, lagging somewhat behind the girls.

"By the way, all the boys are extras I've hired."

According to the prince, his scheme was to pawn off any girls he didn't like to the extras right away. It was almost refreshing how boldly he flaunted what a monster he was.

"...By the way, it seems like there's one old man mixed in among the extras?"

"Apparently Gramps wanted to join in, too."

"Oh, Gramps..."

According to the prince, Gramps had insisted on participating in the grand ball, saying some nonsense about the springtime of his life coming late, or something.

"So what do you think, Miss Witch? Are there any quality girls here?"

"Let me see..."

All the girls that I could see had occupied themselves with the feast laid out on the banquet table the moment the doors opened.

They're like a herd of wild animals, grazing without a care in the world...

Somehow it seemed like there were hardly any girls who had actually come hoping to meet the prince.

Which means...

"There are no girls here who are suitable for you, Your Highness."

Well, frankly speaking, that's what it comes down to. I'm not lying. It's just that their motives for being here are not the same as yours.

"I see…" The prince hung his head. But immediately afterward, his eyes lit up. "No, wait a second, there might just be one!"

Oh? But I can't believe so suddenly that there is anyone so foolish as to want to marry this prince?

"See, over there! Look there!"

My gaze followed where the prince's finger was pointing.

"……"

The girl standing there appeared to be in her late teens. Her hair was the color of ash, and her eyes were lapis. She wore a beautiful white dress, and in one hand she was carrying a rather large bag.

She took no notice of the extravagant meat dishes. Instead, this suspicious girl was shoveling every piece of bread set out on the table into her large bag.

By the way, who on earth was that girl, whom I couldn't help recognizing?

……

To all appearances, she was Elaina.

"That girl looks really great…"

What are you talking about?

"She's no good."

"But why?"

"If I were a betting woman, I'd say that girl loves bread and gold more than any man."

"Well then, why did she come to a place like this?"

"She came to scavenge for bread and gold."

"Wouldn't that make her the worst kind of lowlife?"

"That's why you should give up on pursuing her."

I wasn't lying.

So she did come to the ball after all… But why? I wonder if she really has fallen for the prince? Or maybe, as I just witnessed, she's been lured in by the bread?

I didn't understand her well enough to know her true intention.

"But she sure is cute…"

Oh my, what is he talking about?

"She's a girl who came to your grand ball to steal bread."

"That playful side of her is good, too." Apparently, the prince was not very perceptive. Then he said, "Would you go and speak to her for me?"

"......"

There could be nothing more bothersome, but all right, fine.

"Certainly."

I decided to pretend to follow the prince's orders and stealthily get Elaina out of there.

○

I was completely focused on stealing bread. This stuff had been made for a royal ball, so it was a cut above the loaves you could got from the street stalls in town. It was fluffy and warm, and I felt as if I could go on eating it forever.

This is the good stuff...

In fact, it was so good that I nearly forgot all about the request from the stepmother and her daughters. I almost fled the scene with my spoils right then and there.

"Elaina...don't..."

As I finished stuffing bread into my bag, I heard the echo of a familiar voice from somewhere.

"Elaina...stop doing such a disgraceful thing..."

I turned around, but the voice's owner was nowhere to be seen, and even when I looked around the room, I didn't see anyone watching me.

"......?"

Well now, just what is going on here?

"...Who's there?" I asked.

Somehow, I feel like that voice was similar to Miss Fran's...

"I am your conscience," the voice replied.

"My conscience...?"

"Yes, your conscience, speaking up from inside you, telling you to stop stealing bread from the royal ball…"

……

No, clearly Miss Fran is speaking to me from somewhere; that's the only likely explanation. Maybe she's using magic to project her thoughts directly into my head?

"What are you doing, Miss Fran?"

"You are mistaken. I am your conscience. I am not Fran."

"Unfortunately, my conscience died in battle a long time ago."

"…No, you must have one… Surely even you must have a conscience… There's no way that you really came here just to rob the buffet table."

"Munch, munch."

"Stop eating bread!"

"By the way, Miss Fran, where are you right now? I can't see you."

"I'm watching you from a little ways away— Ah, no, that was a lie, I was joking. I am your conscience," answered Miss Fran, or rather, my conscience, after clearing her throat. "I am speaking to you from inside your heart."

She is really a terrible liar.

"So your job was to come to the ball, was it?"

"Incorrect. I am here to help."

"You are Miss Fran, after all, aren't you?"

"Um…no, you're mistaken. By the way, what are you doing in a place like this? Is it possible that you actually came just to steal bread?"

"If you're my conscience, wouldn't you know why I came here?"

"……"

She was silent.

As I suspected, Miss Fran was apparently somewhere in the hall and had undoubtedly, unmistakably infiltrated the place to do a job, whatever it was.

Well, I'm pretty sure she's not here for the same reasons I am.

"Hey, you. Is my bread delicious?"

Just then, my target appeared suddenly before my eyes. Standing there before me was a young man with lovely golden hair, wearing a carefree smile. There didn't seem to be anything else that was remarkable about him.

"I'm the prince of this country. And you are?"

"Munch, munch."

"Won't you stop eating bread?"

"I'm Elaina. The Ashen Witch," I answered, chomping away.

"Wow, a witch!" The prince seemed happy for some reason. "By the way, being a witch means that you can use all sorts of spells, right?"

"Sure I can; I'm a witch."

"For example, a spell to hit a person with a whip, or a spell to make it hurt three thousand times as badly, or a spell to give someone a really mean look?"

"……"

"Ahh! You don't need to use any spells right away! But hey, that look, those eyes, it's fantastic!"

"……"

He really is something else…

"Elaina…Elaina?" Just then, my conscience (Miss Fran) spoke to me again. "Please, run away… That man is the lowest of the low… He's certainly much worse than you can imagine…"

"Actually, he seems to be pretty much exactly what I expected…"

"Well…! I guess you have no eye for men, then…" For some reason, Miss Fran seemed awfully shocked. Apparently there had been some sort of misunderstanding.

"…Um, I'm not really planning to fall in love with him, or anything…"

"Ah, right, of course not." Miss Fran's voice was cheerful again, as if nothing had happened. "So then why are you here attending the ball?"

"…It's a long story, but I have to get this guy to fall in love with me at all costs."

"……………………………………………………………………………
………………Is that so?"

A heavy silence fell over her.

Apparently, my statement had been misleading.

"To be honest, I'm here on a job," I added.

"Of course."

It concerned me that Miss Fran's voice was devoid of emotion, but I kept talking.

"Apparently there is one weird girl who has fallen deeply in love with this prince. The girl's stepfamily loves her and doesn't want the prince to take her away, so they want me to interfere and prevent them from getting married."

"But even if she came to the ball, isn't it impossible to know whether or not she would win the prince's heart?"

"…I gave the family the same advice, but according to them, this girl likes princes, so the prince is sure to like her back. Apparently."

"I see. That's totally nonsensical."

"…Yep, it sure is."

"But he is a prince, so I suppose it's not impossible that something might happen."

"That's what I thought, too."

The prince was apparently even more obsessed with girls than I had been told.

"Anyway, you're cute," the prince said. "Where do you live? Do you have a boyfriend?"

He didn't seem to have heard one bit of my rather lengthy whispered conversation with Miss Fran. It was honestly pretty amazing.

"…So, Elaina, that means you didn't come here because you've actually fallen for the prince, right? You're just here because you have to be, for a job, right?"

"That's right."

Miss Fran seemed to have already forgotten that she'd been

pretending to be my inner voice. She spoke to me as usual, as my teacher.

"Well, I'm awfully relieved to hear that. I was certain that you had gone into town and fallen carelessly in love…"

"I'm not such an easy girl that I would fall in love at first sight with someone I just met!" I huffed.

"Is that so?" I felt that the emotion had finally come back to Miss Fran's voice. In her usual gentle tone, she said, "But you don't need to impress anybody by sacrificing yourself to try to take down the prince. There's no need for you to go that far."

"……" I decided not to mention the fact that I was going to try to stealthily "borrow" all the valuables while attending the ball.

"Regarding the commission that you accepted, Elaina, there's no real need for you to get the prince to fall for you. I've already got something in the works."

"……?"

I frowned suspiciously.

After a brief silence, Miss Fran's clear voice once again echoed through my head.

"I've arranged for a stand-in."

"…A stand-in?"

"Yes, a stand-in—or rather, I've found a strange girl who actually does like the prince and brought her here. Because in order to satisfy the prince's very specific romantic preferences, a person suitable for the job is absolutely essential," Fran explained.

At that moment, the doors to the hall were thrown open with a bang.

"Th-this is…! The venue for the grand ball…!"

A beautiful girl with golden hair was standing there, wearing a devious smirk. I thought I recognized her face from somewhere.

……

"Miss Fran?"

"Yes?"

I let out a sigh, directed at the teacher who was watching me from somewhere.

"The girl I was hired to protect? That's her."

After bursting into the ball, the girl announced that her name was Lislette, then headed straight for the prince.

○

Let me explain how on earth Miss Fran, who should have had no acquaintance whatsoever with Lislette, ended up bringing her right to the prince.

The two of them had met the morning of the ball.

Miss Fran had accepted the commission from the prince but was feeling dispirited because it was too much of a pain to deal with. So she had gone for a walk around town.

If she didn't do something, the prince was going to hold his ball and probably demand that she somehow make whichever girl struck his fancy fall in love with him somehow, and that certainly would have been a big pain. So it seemed to her that the best plan was to find a girl who was already in love with the prince, lure her to the ball, and set the two of them up together.

And so Miss Fran went searching around town, looking for a girl who would be a good match for the prince.

But it turned out that although all the girls who were planning to attend the ball seemed, at least on the surface, like they were taken with the prince, the truth was that most of them actually showed no interest in him whatsoever. They were all more excited for the free banquet, or the prospect of striking it rich just for pretending to fall in love. Everyone seemed to have their own dishonest reasons for attending the ball. Miss Fran said that it felt like she was dealing with a "whole crowd of Elainas" or something, but we'll set that aside for now.

Anyway, finding a stand-in was rough going. Miss Fran couldn't find even one decent prospect.

"Eh-heh-heh…once I'm done with this job…I can go to the ball… heh-heh…"

Not even a single decent girl.

"……"

Most of the girls in town thought of the ball as nothing more than a chance to fill their stomachs. Anyone actually looking forward to meeting the prince would have been a real outlier.

After wandering around town for a while, Miss Fran apparently spotted a strange girl out doing her shopping while frequently muttering, "I wuv the prince…," and other less intelligible things to herself.

"……"

Immediately after she saw the girl, Miss Fran thought, *Ah, certainly this girl is madly in love with the prince. I see, I see—*

Then, an idea flashed into her mind.

That's it! I'll stick this girl and the prince together.

"Um, excuse me." And so Miss Fran immediately put her hand on the girl's shoulder. "Are you, by chance, in love with the prince?" she asked, so directly it could be called tactless.

Immediately, the girl—Lislette—shrieked in surprise, "Eee! H-how did you…! Who are you…?"

"I'm a witch, just passing through." Miss Fran's words were not untrue. "You looked so troubled, I couldn't just watch, and I decided to say something to you. I am a good witch, you know." That part was mostly made up. "You are in love with the prince, yet you think that your dream of being with him will never be realized… Am I wrong?"

"……"

"If you like, perhaps I could be of assistance?"

"Assist…me…?"

When a suspicious witch suddenly appears out of nowhere and offers to help, most normal people would turn her away. That's probably what I would have done. I might have even spit at her. So it was hard to believe that someone would just obediently nod along to whatever such a stranger proposed.

"Uh...*you*...assist *me*, you say...?"

But Lislette was apparently sort of off in the head, and she immediately agreed.

"...Oh, happy day!" she exclaimed.

At that point in the story, I became very worried that Lislette was going to spend the rest of her life falling for various fishy scams and such, but that's another matter, so let's leave it aside for now.

"Please, attend the royal ball. If you do, I will support you and make sure you're wed to the prince," Miss Fran assured Lislette.

"But...I've got work to do..."

"What work do you have?"

"I've got shopping. My stepmother asked me..." Lislette's stepmother and sisters were planning to keep her busy with too many chores, so that she wouldn't even have the chance to attend the royal ball.

"Oh-hoh, shopping, is it? By the way, where is your house?"

"Over there." Lislette pointed.

"Over there, hm?" Miss Fran waved her wand.

"......" Lislette stared in the direction of her house. Some sort of weird fog descended on her stepfamily's home. "Um, what's that?"

"I've put all the residents in that area to sleep. Now the person who asked you to go shopping is no longer in the picture, you see? So please attend the royal ball."

Miss Fran had brought Lislette's errands to a close in quite a forceful way. That said, all she had done was produce some fog, so she hadn't actually put anyone to sleep, but—

"...Amazing! So this is a witch's power...!"

Since Lislette was a little off anyway, she believed every word that Miss Fran said.

"You'll have to change your clothes, too."

She would need to be appropriately dressed in order to attend the ball. Miss Fran pointed her wand at Lislette next.

Miss Fran had already had her meeting with the prince and had accepted his request. Of course, she was also well informed about the prince's awful fetish, so doing Lislette's makeup and hair so that her appearance matched the prince's tastes was right up her alley.

As Miss Fran waved her wand around effortlessly, Lislette's shabby clothes transformed quickly into a beautiful outfit.

"......"

It was a leather dress in tones of red and black, and sharp high heels. It even had a coiled whip fastened at the hip. She looked less like she was on her way to a ball, and more like she was going to kill someone violently.

The outfit was absolutely not the kind of thing Miss Fran liked.

The day before, the prince had given Miss Fran a piece of paper with a picture on it and told her that he was sure to fall in love with any girl who looked like the girl in the picture. Miss Fran had figured out that the prince was actually just telling her how to dress any girl she presented to him.

The outfit was obviously utterly inappropriate for a royal ball.

"...So apparently the prince likes outfits like this..." It was bad enough that even Miss Fran felt guilty about dressing an innocent young girl in such a getup.

"Mm-mm...don't worry about it..." But Lislette cupped her own chest. "It's really kind of exciting...," she said.

"Uaaagh..."

Ah, this girl seems like a good match for the prince..., Miss Fran apparently thought in her heart of hearts.

And that's how Miss Fran ended up helping Lislette attend the ball.

○

"Which is all to say, I failed utterly at the job you all gave me. I'm sorry."

So I made it through the royal ball, returned to the stepmother and her daughters, and explained the situation to them at length.

I had never imagined that Miss Fran would be operating behind the scenes, so I hadn't foreseen the possibility of failure. There was nothing I could do but apologize.

I prepared myself for the inevitable shower of complaints that I was sure would follow.

But...

"I see, hmm..." The stepmother was unexpectedly calm. "So in other words, our Lislette has become someone's wife..."

Ah, I was wrong; she's not calm at all.

"......" The older sister, who had been listening quietly to the conversation, seemed to react to the word *wife*. "You know, housewife fetishes...are a thing."

What are they talking about? I have no idea what's going on.

"......" The younger sister nodded her approval. "Actually, we can think of it like a new facet to appreciate our big sister Cinderella..."

"You two are so optimistic, it's killing me."

So then, there was no reason for me to even try? That's sure what it seems like.

But as a matter of fact, the prince choosing Lislette as his partner did not seem to have been a bad thing for the country.

Miss Fran and I had stayed in town for a little while after the ball, but we hadn't heard one bit of negative gossip about the prince and Lislette.

Rather, when it came to the prince, people were even saying that he had regained some of his composure as a man.

Now, I wonder why that could be?

"I'm sure that he no longer feels the need to act out, now that he's found his ideal partner," Miss Fran said.

"...How does that work?"

"Nobody wants to reveal their ugly side in front of the person they love, right? Everyone naturally tries to show off in front of their beloved."

"......"

Um, well, when it comes to the prince, I feel like he had nothing but ugly parts to begin with…

"In any case, even that prince is going to do a splendid job from now on…probably…I think."

"…That would be nice…"

Because I'd rather not go through so much trouble the next time I visit.

Miss Fran and I continued chatting as we made our way toward the city gates.

On the way there…

"By the way, Elaina." Miss Fran suddenly looked at me. "What kind of person would you say is your preferred type?"

Oh my…

"What's this, all of a sudden?"

"Oh, I was just wondering what kind of person you might try to show off in front of."

"……"

Someone I would show off for?

After thinking for a little while, I smiled back at Miss Fran.

"That's a secret."

Surely Miss Fran cannot possibly understand my feelings on the matter.

Because unlike her, I am great at keeping secrets.

CHAPTER 5

Familiars

Born on a vast estate, the girl knew almost nothing of the outside world.

She had been a captive on the grounds her whole life. Daughter of the only family of mages in the whole country.

"Listen, child, you are to become the heir to this household," the girl's grandmother told her.

The girl spent her days learning about magic.

Learning how to command familiars.

This especially was part of the girl's obligations as the heir to a distinguished house.

"Ready? Inside the box is a vegetable. Cast a spell of transformation, and turn it into a living creature."

The girl's grandmother was a strict and overbearing teacher, and the girl came to despise her harsh lessons. She didn't want to become a witch in the first place and sometimes even wondered why she had to learn magic at all.

"Inside the box is a mouse. As a test, try turning it into a dog."

"Does this look like a dog to you? When will you ever learn to do real magic?"

"If this is the best you can do, you'll never master your own familiar! You're hopeless!"

Day after day after day after day, the girl kept practicing.

But her efforts were in vain.

Because the girl hated magic from the bottom of her heart.

She loved something altogether different.

"Oh! You want to make bread again?"

The girl's sole pleasure was learning how to make bread from her mother. Every time her mother would go to the kitchen, the girl would follow her and beg to be shown how it was done.

But the truth was that making the bread was nothing more than a bonus.

The girl really just wanted time with her mother.

Because only her mother understood her.

"It's always difficult for you, isn't it? But you'll be all right. I'm sure that someday you will command many splendid familiars," her mother often told her, as if she was trying to convince her. "Your great-grandmother used to always be angry with me, too. But you know, because she was so harsh with me, I learned many spells, and now I can use magic to run the household. Grandma wants you to become splendid, too, so she's being strict with you on purpose—severity is the other face of expectation." The girl's mother stroked her face lovingly as she spoke.

By her side, a wolf with a tawny coat sat wagging its tail. The wolf, which was the mother's familiar, probably felt the same way as its mistress.

The first time the girl saw the outside world was when she was ten years old.

To celebrate her birthday, her mother took her into town. The world full of people seemed to sparkle and shine in the eyes of the girl who knew nothing but the inside of her family's mansion.

In town, the people fawned over the girl's mother because of her magical abilities. The girl's mother and grandmother were the only people who could use magic in the area, so whenever either of them left the estate, people would make all sorts of requests of them.

They would be asked to mend broken cups, or find lost items, or fulfill other insignificant requests that might ordinarily be laughed off.

But the girl's mother smiled kindly at the townspeople, and replied, "Yes, of course," and listened to each of their requests.

The girl admired her mother deeply. She wished that someday she could be just like her.

Then one day, while the girl and her mother were walking through town, something happened. After checking that there was no one around them, the girl's mother whispered to her, "To tell you the truth, when I was about your age, I also hated learning spells. Just like you. Long ago, I wondered why I had to suffer and learn magic."

"……"

"But you know, I realized why once I grew up. All the hard work paid off, and now I have the power to help other people in need."

The girl's mother told her that she would have to overcome the hardship of learning, so that she could become strong and capable of helping people, too.

"……"

But the girl responded with silence. It wasn't that she didn't understand. It was just that she didn't believe it. She didn't believe that she could ever become a strong woman like her mother.

She stared up at her mother, who stroked her hair kindly. "...I'm sorry, dear. You're only ten years old. It must be so difficult for you."

In addition, her mother told her one more secret. "When you're feeling down, you can leave the estate by yourself. If you learn about the outside world, I think you, too, will surely come to appreciate magic a little bit more."

"...But..."

Leaving the estate by herself had always been strictly prohibited. The only time the girl had ever seen the outside world was when she was at her mother's side.

The only thing that had ever been permitted for the girl was magical training—such was her unpleasant life on the estate.

"Try pushing your way through a certain bush about thirty paces to the right of the front gate. There's a small hole in the fence there." The girl's mother stealthily explained to her that she could get out that way. "You know, your mama was actually a naughty kid back in the day!"

She taught her daughter one method to become more like her.

After that, the girl started escaping outside the grounds whenever she had free time.

Even though she knew it was bad, even though just thinking about what punishments awaited her if her grandmother ever found out was terrifying, even so, as soon as the girl had snuck out once, she became numb to that fear and started slipping away from the mansion more often.

The town looked quite different alone, compared to when she'd had her mother by her side. This new, lonely world seemed awfully vast, and shining with promise. But at the same time, she could also see darkness. The girl soon realized that her mother had kept to the larger, more crowded, and safer parts of town.

There were lots of people in the city. There were lots of animals, too.

The girl learned that she was by no means the only unhappy one.

She saw adults who had failed to do their jobs and who were being reprimanded harshly. She saw people sleeping by the side of the road, who had no homes to live in. She saw stray dogs, rummaging through trash cans for food. She saw a mouse that had gotten caught in a trap and was dying.

In a back alley, covered in blood and close to death, she saw a tiny creature.

"……"

That was the first meeting between the girl and her familiar.

She had been born on a vast estate, but sure enough, she knew almost nothing about the outside world.

"…The same dream again."

The girl rubbed her eyes and looked around. The world seemed like it was filled with light. On top of the table, dense reference tomes were piled up like a mountain. Nearby lay a pen and an unfinished document.

Apparently, she had fallen asleep in the middle of writing.

Partway through the text, the letters devolved into clumsy lines, dampened by tears and sweat. They were completely illegible.

"......"

Filled with frustration, the girl crumpled the paper up into a ball and tossed it to the floor. There was no one there to chide her for doing so. This was her private room.

Besides that, there were no longer any humans in the mansion, other than the girl.

Half a year earlier, everyone else had disappeared from the estate.

They had left her behind and passed away.

There was no one around to criticize the girl, no matter how dirty her room got, no matter how untidy she was.

Almost as if possessed, she muttered to herself.

"Harder... I've got to work harder..."

Then the girl took up her pen once again.

○

"Are the two of you in possession of any familiars?"

A government official had taken us aside as we were waiting to enter Ballad, the City of Silence. She had told us only that she had something important to discuss, then invited us into a separate room near the city gate, locked the door, and tossed out that question.

Familiars?

"I don't have any." Miss Fran shook her head.

"Same here." I nodded.

To begin with, magic users can manage to handle most situations by themselves, so there aren't many circumstances where we would need to use familiars. These days, you could even say cultivating familiars is more like an old-fashioned, traditional hobby, and it's rare to see mages who keep one on hand.

"Is that so…?"

But the government official's expression grew cloudy at our answers. *What's this now?*

"By any chance, are you saying that we can't enter the city if we don't have familiars? Not only do we not have any, but I hardly even have the knowledge to use them in the first place…"

What a pain.

We'll be in trouble if we can't get in the city… We'll have to camp out.

But my concern was nothing more than unfounded worry. The official shook her head.

"No, you'll be permitted to enter regardless of whether or not you have any familiars. The reason I summoned you here has nothing to do with customs."

"Well then, why?" Miss Fran asked the obvious question.

The official's expression didn't change much as she told us, "The only family of mages in the area has employed familiars for ages. Generation after generation, down to the present head of the family, they have inherited the tradition. We have a request for the two of you regarding this family—no, regarding an issue that is troubling the city."

She held out a piece of paper in front of us.

It was a request form to be submitted to the United Magic Association. In the section for remuneration was an amount of gold coin based on the estimated total cost of all food and lodging for the period of stay in Ballad, the City of Silence.

It was a considerable sum.

Enough to take my breath away.

"I'd like to ask you to undertake the job, with the conditions that are listed here."

But if they were offering substantial remuneration, that could only mean one thing.

The problem itself was equally substantial.

"...What on earth happened here?" Miss Fran held the paper up.

I glanced at the paper from the side and read only, *Seizure of Familiars*.

"One of the familiars employed by the family went on a rampage and murdered almost every one of them, sparing only its mistress, a young girl. Now the wild familiar is appearing around the city, threatening people's daily lives... This is a local problem, so we're terribly ashamed of asking for help from travelers, but..."

The family that had been using the familiars had been completely annihilated, leaving only one girl, the mistress of the murderer.

Which means...

"There was only one mage left alive."

...that the very person who let the familiar carry out its rampage is the only one left.

And presumably the girl wasn't a capable enough magic user to stop her family's murder. So that was why this official had turned to me and Miss Fran, even though we were travelers.

From the official's perspective, we had arrived at exactly the right time.

"......"

Miss Fran was silent as she stared down at the piece of paper.

So from beside her, I asked, "What is the girl's name?"

The government official looked at me and answered with a single word.

Karen.

That was the name of the pitiful girl, the only one left on the estate.

○

I could smell the faint aroma of saltwater wafting throughout the city.

As we looked down the gently sloping road, the glaring light reflecting off the ocean's surface was dazzling. The city extended right down to the water's edge.

We were approaching the end of Miss Fran's journey. She had plans to return to Royal Celestelia by boat.

"It showed up right after sunrise. My pet dog suddenly started barking, so I looked out the window to the garden, wondering what was going on, and there it was. It looked disgusting."

Miss Fran had immediately accepted the official's request, and I had agreed to join her on the investigation.

We'd been going around randomly speaking to people we passed in town, and we had discovered that apparently Karen's familiar had been causing quite a lot of trouble for the people in the city.

We heard countless eyewitness reports.

"My shop's garbage cans were broken into. It somehow removed the lids and picked out anything that still seemed edible from the cans. I know it's not really serious damage, but…"

They said that the familiar took the form of an animal. Its coat was black. Its eyes were green. Its fangs were sharp, and its claws were filthy. Apparently, its form resembled a wolf in some respects, but more than anything, its build was enormous, and it was about as long as a grown man is tall.

"It seems to like bread. It used to come to my shop often and stare hungrily at the bread. I can easily chase off the homeless kids that I always see hanging around, but that thing, I mean, it's huge! And I've got a little daughter at home, so it scared the living daylights out of me, thinking it might hurt me."

We heard that the beast rarely appeared to humans, but since it had apparently been lured in by its favorite food—bread—we decided that it couldn't be especially intelligent.

But the question was why a creature like this had been ignored by the people of the city for half a year? If it was so repulsive, a ghastly monster that destroyed crops and went rummaging through garbage cans, then why on earth had no one dealt with it yet?

A guard on his rounds was kind enough to answer this extremely natural question for us.

"We've tried to capture it many times before, but it didn't work. We even recruited help from the townspeople and chased the beast down with everything we could muster, but…that wolf is very fast. There's absolutely no way that ordinary people could ever hope to catch it, not without magic," the guard told us with a sigh. "It would be great if we could turn to our own mage for help, but…"

He explained.

Ever since the death of her family, Karen, the mistress of the familiar, had isolated herself in her estate. She had stopped leaving the place altogether.

Many people in the city felt like they owed Karen's family for their help in the past, while others took pity on the poor girl and her awful circumstances. Some people occasionally went to check on her and left food for her, but not one of them had actually seen Karen in person.

At this point, no one knew whether she was alive or dead behind the closed gates.

"…Where is that estate located?"

The guard nodded to me and pointed to an enormous mansion at the other end of town.

Since we knew the characteristics of the rogue familiar and had a rough estimate of its territory, we figured that was sufficient.

Next, we planned to search the mages' estate, then hunt down the familiar's whereabouts, and then finally, head to find Karen…into the mansion where the girl whom we had never even seen was holed up. That seemed like the thing to do if we hoped to resolve the affair quickly and decisively.

In any case…

"Um, first let me get one of the chef's special salads, and a cup of your cheapest coffee, and then all of the bread from here to there. That's my whole order."

I promptly slammed the menu book shut.

Miss Fran and I were sitting across from each other at one of the city's cafés. We had more or less finished interviewing witnesses for the day. A member of the waitstaff had come to take our order, so I had done something I'd always wanted to do, and asked for all the bread from here to there.

"Is it all right to ask for so much?" Miss Fran tilted her head questioningly beside the waiter, who was hurriedly jotting down my order on a memo pad.

There was no cause for concern. After all…

"The city is covering all of our food expenses, yaaay!"

As long as someone else is paying, there's no problem ordering exactly what I want, right?

The unexpected boon was messing with my head and leading me to make some odd choices. Miss Fran, on the other hand, was as reserved as always.

"Ah, I'm fine with a cup of tea," she said to the waiter.

How modest.

"But is it all right, Elaina? An order like that?"

After the waiter had left, Miss Fran leaned forward and whispered the question at me.

She was probably worried about whether I would be able to eat all of it by myself.

"No need to worry. This is the kind of upright café that allows carryout."

"No, that's not what I mean." Miss Fran shook her head in exasperation. "Is the *cost* all right?"

"It's someone else's money, so I really don't care."

The government is covering the full cost of our meals as long as we're in the city. No matter how much money we spend while we're here, as long as we get receipts, we'll get it all back. What are you worried about?

"But if we mess up the job, we won't be getting any money, you know."

"…!"

"I mean, that's just common sense."

"……………………………………………………………………..I knew that!"

"I'm letting you know this in advance. I'm not paying for you, okay?"

"Miss Fran, under no circumstances can we fail to fulfill the city's request!"

"Now there's something I might have liked to hear you say once or twice before…"

Only after the risk of having to pay my own way for everything had come up, and before I had time to cancel my order, the waiter brought over everything we had ordered, all together.

At that point, it was too late to do anything. Hanging my head, I stopped him before he could leave. "Um, sorry, but…could I get a bag for takeout? A big one, if possible."

With a puzzled face, the waiter brought me a bag.

I packed all the bread into it, sobbing the whole time.

Miss Fran watched me vacantly and took a sip of tea. Then, as if she had just remembered it, she said, "When we leave this café, we'll be going to Karen's place, of course."

"……" After getting my bread bag together, I nodded. "Yes, of course."

Frankly speaking, neither Miss Fran nor I had much experience with familiars.

If we were able to stop the rogue familiar with the help of its mistress, Karen, then we would do that, and if she couldn't leave her mansion for some reason, then we would need to determine what that reason was.

There was no way to do either without meeting her.

But if we were going to meet someone…

"From here on, it would be best if you and I took different paths, Miss Fran."

"Right," my teacher said. "We don't know what kind of state Karen might be in, but she hasn't left her mansion in half a year, so we can be quite certain that she's got some reason for that."

Since Karen had lost her family, and on top of that, the familiar that was supposed to belong to her had been causing so much trouble in the city, it was hard to imagine that she was just up there relaxing with too much time on her hands, completely unbothered.

Maybe she's closed up her heart just like the doors to her house?

If that was true, we still needed to go meet her and talk to her. But although we'd been traveling together, it seemed to me that if both of us showed up uninvited at her door, could she really be expected to open her heart to us?

Probably not.

"I'll go alone to Karen's place."

According to the government official, Karen was a little bit younger than I was.

I figured that if one of us was going to head up to her mansion, I would be more suitable, as I was comparatively closer in age.

"I'll leave it to you." Miss Fran nodded. "Meanwhile, I'll chase down the familiar's whereabouts."

And then, not long after we'd stopped to rest, we stood up from our chairs.

Right as we left the café, Miss Fran proposed, "I've got to go make a reservation at a hotel, too. Let's meet up at the end of the day and both report on our progress."

I see, I see.

"Please choose a cheap place."

"Let's stay somewhere expensive."

"Miss…"

"We can split the cost, all right?"

"Miss……"

In the end, after much badgering and quarreling, it was decided that we would be staying in a reasonably expensive inn.

This means that we have to fulfill the city's request, by any means necessary...

○

"Excuuuse meee! Your gate was open, so I came on in! Is anyone heeere?!"

Well, now.

On an estate somewhere, there was a mage who, after using a spell to easily open the lock on a gate that had been shut tight, made a shameless introduction as she casually committed criminal trespassing.

Who on earth could this girl be, who didn't hesitate at all to commit such a blatantly illicit act?

That's right, it's me.

"...Huh, there's no answer."

I wonder what that means. I made my entrance pretty obvious.

As I pondered this, I walked toward the huge mansion that towered before me.

I wasn't particularly worried about one girl, especially because we weren't even sure if she was alive or dead, so I also unlocked the mansion doors easily with another spell.

"......"

Unlike the stately exterior, the inside of the place had fallen into ruin.

A chandelier that must have once hung from the ceiling lay pitifully on the red-carpet runner, sparkling fragments scattered all around the floor. The paintings hanging on the walls were black with filth, and the staircase was riddled with holes. The place looked like a storm had blown through.

Whenever I took a step, chandelier fragments crunched and snapped underfoot.

Karen must be somewhere in this house.

"Hellooo?"

I didn't really know which way to go in order to find her, so I walked around aimlessly, exploring the house and shouting greetings into empty space.

After trekking through the mansion for a while, I eventually came to an area of the house where there were no glass shards underfoot. Instead, the place was littered with balls of scrap paper.

When I picked one up and smoothed out the wrinkles, the scrap of paper revealed rows of messy writing.

After that, I picked the papers up one by one as I walked.

Eventually, the pieces of paper led me deep into the mansion—to a door that was slightly ajar.

"……"

Inside was a spacious room, in terrible disarray.

The balls of rubbish that had spread out into the hallways were scattered liberally across the floor of the room and on top of the bed, and here and there across the walls, overlapping papers were held up by pushpins.

The sound of the creaking door echoed through the quiet space, where an open curtain swayed in the sunlight, and the gentle breeze that flowed in turned the pages of a book that sat spread open on the desk.

The girl who was facedown in front of the book frowned slightly and sat up. Her golden hair went down past her shoulders, and her robe was decorated all over and looked incredibly expensive. She certainly appeared to be the daughter of a noble family.

In age, she was probably about two or three years younger than me. There was still youth in her features. She finally noticed me standing beside the door and turned her head in my direction.

Her eyes looked dull, and I could see faint, dark circles beneath them.

"…Who?"

She made an expression that looked halfway between enraged suspicion and unbearable drowsiness and tilted her head to the side.

I wasn't sure how to answer her.

"I'm a traveling witch."

I offered the briefest of introductions.

"I came here to put a stop to the trouble your familiar is causing in the city," I added.

"……"

I wasn't sure what she made of what I said. She just stared at me silently, with no change in her expression.

Surely she must be aware of the strange things that are happening around town.

Maybe she felt responsible for what was going on. Maybe she was worried about it. I was sure that she had to be in a more difficult position than anyone in town. So I stood there waiting for her to say something.

"Trespassing."

That was it.

"……"

She was unexpectedly calm.

●

After Elaina and I had gone our separate ways, I heard all sorts of stories from the residents of the town, but there didn't really seem to be anyone who had any promising leads.

Apparently, the people who lived in town had seen the familiar many times, but they had absolutely no way of guessing where or when the elusive creature might appear next.

I was at a loss.

But my meandering hadn't been a complete waste of time.

"…What's this?"

Just as I was thinking that there was no way I'd run into the familiar by chance, I happened upon something very strange in the back alleys of the city. I had no way of knowing whether or not it had anything to do with the familiar.

Right in the middle of a dirty alleyway, placed neatly atop a small plate, was a single piece of abandoned bread.

"......"

What's this, lost and found? But it's sitting on a plate for some reason. I feel like it was clearly left here intentionally. Wait, wait, this has got to be a trap.

"My goodness..."

When I looked up, I saw another piece of bread farther down the alley.

That was approximately when even I, as clueless as I am, noticed that the plates with bread sitting on them continued endlessly down the alley.

"My, what a waste...!"

I picked them up one by one and stuffed them in my bag.

I've never seen anything so absurd. Surely this must be a trap that has been laid out in order to catch the familiar. In that case, the person who came up with the strategy to waste all this bread probably ought to be lying in wait at the end of the trail.

I believe I know of someone who purchased such a huge quantity of bread recently.

Actually, I was just with her.

"Elaina...unbelievable."

If I'm not mistaken, she should be on her way to Karen, but...what on earth is she up to? Actually, it's outrageous to think that she would come up with a strategy like this that wastes so much food!

And so I walked along collecting pieces of bread, so that I could scold Elaina, who I assumed was lying in wait at the end of this ridiculous trap.

After proceeding on for a little while, I reached the final piece of bread.

The bread had been laid out nicely on plates the whole way, but the last piece was in an unusual place.

It was hanging suspended beneath a streetlight.

©Azure

Moreover, it had been dusted abundantly in a mysterious white powder.

Too suspicious…

I wasn't sure whether eating the bread would knock you out or just paralyze you, but it was quite clear that there was something off about it. The trap was just too obvious. But I was certain that no harm would come to me, as long as I didn't eat it.

So I pulled the last piece of bread toward me and took it in my hand.

"Elaina, where—aaah!"

—are you? Come out now. Jeez. That's what I was about to say. But the rest of the words didn't make it out of my mouth. Instead, halfway through, they were cut off by an immodest scream.

"……"

The trap sprang into action as soon as I tugged on the last piece of bread. Before I realized what was happening, I was suspended below the streetlight just as the last piece of bread had been a moment earlier.

Both arms were pinned near my hips, and both legs were restrained along with my skirts. I was completely helpless, just swaying slowly back and forth under the lamp.

Nothing could have been more wretched.

And then…

Just as flames of shame and humiliation were about to erupt from my face, the person responsible for catching me in the trap stepped out of hiding.

Is it Elaina? It must be Elaina. There's no one else it could be—that's what I thought, until I saw her face.

"I never thought you would be that easy to catch. You may be a familiar, but in the end, you're still just a dog."

Standing there was a witch…but it wasn't Elaina.

She wore a white robe and a white triangular hat, and upon her breast she wore both a star-shaped brooch and a moon-shaped brooch with pride. Her hair was golden blond, and she was about the same age as me.

"......" She studied my face, frozen in place, her pipe dangling from her mouth.

"......" For my part, I was already physically immobilized, ever since I had been strung up.

Now, if I had stopped to think about it, I would have realized that since there was an organization in the world whose very purpose was dealing with magical disturbances, it was probably pretty likely that the government here had already reached out to that group before asking a couple of wanderers for help. And that it was also fairly likely that another mage had already been dispatched from the United Magic Association.

And so...

...the face before me was a very familiar one.

I was looking at my fellow former apprentice, Sheila.

"...What're you doing?" she demanded coldly before blowing smoke in my direction.

"...What does it look like I'm doing?"

"Something stupid."

"......" I stared at her silently.

"......" Sheila stared silently back.

"......" Eventually, I looked away. "Um, first of all, could I get you to let me down?"

Sheila nodded solemnly. "And afterward, we can go get something to eat together. My treat."

"Stop that. Don't talk down to me," I huffed.

"If you're strapped for cash, come and talk to me. I'll help you out if you need it."

"Seriously, stop it—you've got it all wrong anyway—this is..."

"Sure, sure. Of course I'll keep quiet about it to your pupil. Even she would feel sad if she knew that her esteemed teacher was eating off the street."

"Oh, there's no issue there. Elaina's had her fill of watching me do that."

It made me sad to admit it.
Why am I telling her that?
"......" Sheila made an extremely complicated face, then clapped a hand down on my shoulder. "We can go get something to eat together. My treat."
"Stop that. Don't talk down to me."

○

"I figured someone would come sooner or later," the girl said after glancing at the brooch on my breast. Maybe she didn't have enough strength left to turn me, the trespasser, away. Or maybe she allowed me in because she could tell I was a witch.

With an expression like she understood everything already, she said, "I suppose you've come to kill me?"

"......"

No, you don't understand a thing, do you...?

The girl probably had no idea what I was doing there.

"No, um...not at all?"

Why would you suddenly jump to such a disturbing idea? Are you so tired that you're ready to die?

"I just came to talk...," I insisted.

"And you're planning to kill me after we talk? You mustn't. Please, I must ask you to wait a little longer before killing me."

No, I'm telling you, I didn't come here to kill you, Karen...

And anyway...

"Even supposing that I did sneak into your mansion intent on killing you, I would have finished the job while you were taking your afternoon nap."

"...!"

"What about that is surprising?"

Karen looked unusually confused. Fatigue must have been sapping her wits. The bags under her eyes told me that she hadn't been sleeping much lately.

"All right, so if you didn't come to kill me, what did you come here for?"

"I think I said this already, but..." I figured I would repeat myself. "...I came here to put a stop to the trouble your familiar is causing in the city."

"......"

Karen listened to my words, and then glanced quickly behind and around me, then cocked her head and asked, "Miss Witch, do you not have a familiar?"

"As you can see, I do not."

"So your knowledge of familiars is...?"

"Rather poor, unfortunately."

"So you don't really know what you have to do to stop a familiar?"

"Well, I suppose when you put it that way..."

That's why I came to see you. If I had known why you abandoned your familiar and locked yourself in here, and how to stop a familiar to begin with, I wouldn't have bothered breaking in.

"I see."

Karen nodded curtly.

Either she was a naturally stoic person or just deadened by exhaustion. She kept her gaze fixed to the ground and didn't make eye contact as she began to fill me in little by little.

"The word *familiar* describes an animal that has been imbued with magical power. When a familiar goes rogue, there are two ways to stop it. One is to dissolve the connection it has to its master. If you do that, the familiar will revert to its original form. It's even possible to stop my familiar from threatening the city that way."

Well, how about doing that, then?

The heartless words made it into my throat before I stopped them.

Karen has stayed shut up in her house despite knowing a way to stop the familiar, which must mean that it is not an easy method.

As far as I could see anyway, the girl before me now did seem to be moping around all heartbroken.

"What can you do to dissolve that connection?" I asked.

"What will you do if I tell you?" Karen asked me in return.

"Help you do it."

"I don't need your help," Karen insisted briskly. "This is my problem. It's got nothing to do with you. Besides, even if you do help me, I can't compensate you in return."

Well, if it's a question of payment, there's a chance I can squeeze plenty out of someone else, so you don't need to worry about that.

"If you wouldn't feel right without paying me somehow, you can tell me the sequence of events that led to your familiar's rampage. How about that?"

"...Why are you so insistent on helping me?"

"Because you seemed to be feeling awkward about not being able to pay me."

"I don't really feel awkward about it. It's simply that it's my fault that my familiar is causing so much trouble, so if I don't resolve the situation myself, it won't mean anything."

"You mean you want to accept the full responsibility for the disaster you caused?"

"That's it exactly."

I see, I see.

A sigh slipped out of my mouth.

"Well, I have to ask you to save that tiresome way of thinking for later," I said. "You can take all the responsibility you want for releasing your familiar onto the city after we resolve the problem. We've got to get it done, no matter what it takes."

"......" She stared at me silently for a short while.

And then, finally, Karen tilted her head and asked, "And I'm supposed to trust you, a witch I just met?"

"It's fine if you don't particularly want to trust me. But at least let me help, please. At the very least, it'll be far more effective than continuing to sit at your desk by yourself," I replied.

"......"

Karen answered with only silence. She glanced once out the window, then looked at a picture frame that was standing on her desk. After that, she spoke very reluctantly, and said, "...Understood. Then, I will make use of you."

But before I began the long work of reverting the familiar back to its original form, another thought occurred to me.

"That reminds me, what was the other method for stopping a familiar?"

How on earth can we stop it, other than by dissolving the bond it has with you?

Karen answered flatly, without looking at me.

"The death of the master," she said.

If the master dies, so does the familiar...

I realized why there were no familiars left in the mansion.

●

"How long have you been here?"

We were in the alley.

I asked Sheila the question with a composed expression, as if nothing strange had occurred in the past few moments. She tapped a bit of ash out of her pipe onto the ground nearby and answered, "I was dispatched to this city about a week ago. You?"

"I just got here today. I happen to be visiting, along with my pupil, Elaina. We were asked to help capture a familiar."

"......" The moment she heard Elaina's name, a slightly strange expression surfaced on Sheila's face, and she nodded. "I see."

"...What?"

"No, nothing."

Ah, come to think of it...

"Is your pupil Saya getting on well?"

"...Recently, she's—no, that's not something to discuss now."

"......?"

"More importantly, you could say that my objective and yours are more or less the same, huh?"

"Yes, though I would be grateful for any help you could give us."

"Sure, as long as you don't interfere with my next plan."

"Oh, did I get in your way or something? Oh-hoh-hoh!"

I don't remember that at all.

"......"

Sheila screwed her face up into a very, very crude expression.

At any rate, I then revealed to Sheila that I had basically been gathering information since my arrival in the city. I also revealed that Elaina was, at that very moment, heading up to the mage's estate.

"Hmm." Sheila nodded slightly, as if she didn't care. "So you left it up to her to make friends with the familiar's mistress?"

"Yes. Its capture has been left up to us, though."

The familiar's whereabouts were still unknown. We didn't know anything about where it was or even what it was doing.

"Have you gotten any results after being here a week?" I asked.

"For now, I know that the familiar likes bread," Sheila answered.

"Ah, so you interviewed witnesses for your investigation." Elaina and I had also obtained that information. "And? Anything else?"

"Apparently it won't eat bread that has fallen on the ground."

"......"

"What else?"

"That's all."

"That's all?"

But I already knew that, and I've been here less than a day...

"That's how hard this thing is to pin down. I've been looking everywhere for a week, and in the end I still haven't laid eyes on it once."

"......"

So that's why you resorted to desperate measures like leaving bread out in the middle of the road... Well, the only thing you caught was me, though.

Sheila scratched her head in irritation and spit out, "...For something that pops up all over the place, it doesn't seem to be anywhere at all. It's a real troublesome dog."

"My, my. If it can appear anywhere, then maybe if you wait for it, it will simply show up sooner or later."

Let's think positively about this.

"You think I'd be having so much trouble if it was really that easy?"

As Sheila was speaking, her eyes turned in the direction of the lamppost where I had been strung up a few moments earlier.

A moment later, I looked, too.

It seemed like something was moving over there.

"......"

At that exact moment, I remembered something.

I remembered that, earlier, I had collected all the bread that Sheila had scattered down the alleyway, placing each piece one by one in my bag. But when I'd reached out for the last piece and gotten strung up in midair, I had carelessly dropped that bag on the ground. Then Sheila had appeared, so I had completely forgotten about the existence of the bread.

I recalled that fact right at that moment.

The moment that I spotted a familiar holding my bag in its mouth.

"......" Sheila stiffened.

"......" Naturally, I stiffened as well.

I was surprised that the familiar had suddenly appeared from out of nowhere, but more than anything else, I was surprised by its appearance.

It seemed that the rumors hadn't been exaggerated.

Its coat was black. Its eyes were green. Its fangs were sharp, and its claws were filthy. Its form did resemble a wolf in some respect, but more than anything, it was enormous—about as long as a grown man was tall. Sure enough, it was huge, just like the rumors said.

But one thing, one single thing, was completely different from the rumors.

The familiar was all skin and bones.

I could tell even through its black coat. Its limbs were as slender as twigs, its tail drooped, and its paws trembled on the ground. I knew right away that it had to be starving. And yet it didn't eat the bread that was before its eyes. Holding the bag in its mouth, not so much as looking our way—it probably didn't even have the extra energy to look at us—the familiar jumped up on top of the roof of a nearby house and disappeared, dragging one leg behind it.

All we could do was stand there doubting our eyes at the astonishingly sudden sight.

I wondered if a creature in such a weakened state could really have been threatening the people of the city.

"…Hey." Sheila finally looked back at me. "Shouldn't we chase after it?"

"…I suppose we should."

I nodded and pulled out my broom.

We finally had a lead on the rogue familiar. We weren't about to let it get away.

Apparently, we were going to have to investigate just where the creature had been and what it had been doing before now, before it got so thin.

As we followed the familiar, I thought that it looked very, very frail.

○

According to Karen…

When an animal made a pact to become a familiar, it was infused with magic and took on a new form. It became a servant, made to obey any order from its master and carry out any task.

Once master and servant were tied to each other, the familiar gained the ability to borrow magical energy from the mage, and its physical abilities improved as its form changed. Additionally, it gained the power to cast spells, and grew more intelligent, even gaining the ability to speak. Those were generally the kinds of changes that appeared, Karen said.

But it was important to remember that the changes applied only so long as the compact was valid.

So then, if the compact failed, what would happen? Karen answered my extremely reasonable question while she read over some documents.

"Usually, when a pact fails, it happens before the transformation. And in most cases, it results in death at the moment of failure."

"......"

I feel like that is a slightly different circumstance than the present situation with the rogue familiar. Because actually, right now, that familiar is out walking freely around town.

"If a familiar goes wild after a compact has been formed, then the worst possible thing happens," Karen said. "That's what happened to my familiar."

"What happens to them when they go wild?"

"They go into a temporary frenzy, and often injure or even kill anyone nearby."

"......"

That seemed to be what Karen was dealing with now, as she continued her research in isolation.

"You said 'temporary,' meaning that their rampage must end at some point, right?" I asked. "What happens to them once it's over?"

"They are no longer bound to follow their master's orders. They act only on their own intentions."

That probably described Karen's familiar at the moment. Halfway bound by pact, but no longer under its mistress's command, the familiar had been prowling around the city.

One of two means could be used to dissolve the compact.

Either Karen had to die, or the defective pact had to be broken.

Karen told me that she had suffered a setback when she first started searching for a method to rescind the master-servant pact. No matter what she tried, she hadn't been able to make the magical potion she needed to do it.

Although she had inherited all kinds of books on magic along with her estate, the recipe for a potion that would dissolve the pact between mage and familiar was not recorded in any of them.

The idea of doing so had probably been unthinkable to any of the people who had lived in the house before her.

"I've been researching the problem for half a year, but it hasn't been going well."

All she had done was cover the floor in scraps of paper, with nothing to show for it. Sparing almost no time for sleep, she had found it incredibly difficult to try to fumble her way through the magical tomes.

She had studied, made up a recipe for a potion, mixed it, failed, then repeated the process nearly every day. Over and over, she had done it again and again, only to fail each time, destroying the inside of the mansion in the process. The chandelier had fallen, the paintings had gotten filthy, and still, she had repeated her experiments many times.

"……" I picked up the documents that were sitting on her desk. "I understand the circumstances now. First of all, please give me all of the potion recipes you still have on hand."

"But all the ones I mixed were failures—"

"But if I mix them, we might get different results."

"…Understood." Karen nodded reluctantly.

After I took the recipes from her, I started comparing the documents in my hands.

I don't know anything when it comes to familiars, but all my other knowledge and experience should amount to something.

So I sat down beside her, facing the desk just like she was.

"……"

"……"

Both of us remained absolutely silent as I ran pen over paper in fits and starts and discarded scraps of paper by tossing them behind my back.

We forgot the time and sat there all day until the sun set.

The hours passed quietly.

"...Come to think of it, was that familiar originally a dog?"

It suddenly occurred to me to ask, as I was reading over documents.

"Why do you ask...?" Karen looked over her shoulder suspiciously.

"Oh, just because I heard a rumor that its appearance is like a wolf."

Although it wasn't like I had ever actually seen the familiar, so I only had the gossip I'd collected to go on. My rough guess was that if a dog got bigger, it would pretty much look like a wolf. It was almost too simple.

"Wrong."

And apparently my rough guess missed the mark.

"Completely wrong."

Apparently, it was a total miss. Karen shook her head so strongly that her hair swayed. "You can turn your familiar into any form you like. Once the bond between master and servant is formed, the familiar can become anything at all."

Well, from what Karen says, it sounds like transformation magic is a big part of creating a familiar, so I suppose it makes sense that it would take on a new form during the process.

Karen pushed herself away from the desk and turned around.

"My family lineage has raised wolf familiars for generations, so my familiar also took the shape of a wolf, that's all."

So in that case...

"All right, so what kind of animal was it to begin with?"

I was just asking out of curiosity.

I was sort of interested, that's all.

"......"

In response to my completely natural question, Karen hesitated, looked bewildered, and her eyes began to waver.

I must have asked something that I shouldn't have. I had made a mistake. I felt uncomfortable at the strange way she was acting.

"My familiar is…"

And then, after a brief hesitation, she answered.

●

The familiar, still clutching the bag of bread in its mouth, eventually led us to the ruin of a small factory on the outskirts of town. There were no signs of people, and it wasn't hard to understand how no one would have noticed the familiar hiding out in a place like that.

On top of that, the familiar got around by bounding across the rooftops.

"It's hardly surprising that people say it appears out of nowhere, huh?" Sheila nodded to herself, hiding in the shadows so as not to be noticed by the familiar. "No one pays any attention to their rooftops."

"…Yes, indeed." I nodded, too, observing the familiar from a distance.

The wolf with the black fur alighted from a rooftop and headed straight for a small hut that stood in one corner of the ruined factory.

There was no hesitation in its gait. It didn't look tired either, even though it was so unsteady, it had barely been standing a short while ago.

The familiar just walked slowly toward the hut.

"What should we do? Capture it?"

Sheila pulled out her wand and looked at me. Compared to earlier when the creature had been moving around, it seemed like it would be easy to apprehend with magic.

"……"

I didn't answer. Watching the familiar's actions from afar, I just kept silent.

There was a great deal of food lying around the hut in front of the familiar.

There were fruits and vegetables and bread—plenty of food just sitting there. The familiar set the bag of bread that it was carrying down on top of the pile and stood motionless.

It didn't eat any of the food.

It's probably been bringing food here like this for a long time. Even from afar, I could see the remains of the food that had been strewn about in front of the hut, as if someone, or something, was inside.

"...What's it doing?"

"......"

Again, I didn't answer.

But one thing I could have said without a doubt was that even if we didn't capture the familiar today, or tomorrow, or the next day, if we kept on waiting, the familiar was certain to return to this place.

There was no need for us to try to capture it right away.

Before long, the familiar took its leave from that place. Just like when it had arrived, it moved slowly and weakly toward town.

"......"

"......"

In the end, we didn't capture the familiar. But it didn't matter. We knew that we would have many more chances, even if we didn't force ourselves to act on that occasion.

It turned out that our decision was the right one.

Immediately after the familiar left, small figures came crawling out from inside the hut.

Clad in tattered scraps of cloth, three little girls came out, checking their surroundings.

○

That evening, when I went back to the hotel, Miss Fran and Sheila were waiting for me.

They told me about how Miss Fran had run into Sheila in town, and how Sheila was working toward the same goal as we were.

Moreover...

"In the meantime, we've got a general grasp on the familiar's movements. We can capture it at any time," Miss Fran told me hopefully, without hesitation.

But...

"......"

I wasn't exactly happy about the news.

Even if they could capture the familiar, I didn't want them to. For Karen's sake, and for the familiar's sake.

"How did things go for you?" Miss Fran tilted her head.

I answered frankly, "I'm now working with Karen to make a magic potion. Once we perfect her potion, we should be able to return the familiar to its original form."

At my words, Sheila nodded. "Is that so? Then, what kind of animal was that familiar originally?" she asked, staring at me. "I don't suppose it was any ordinary beast."

"......"

I kept silent as the two of them told me about the spectacle they had witnessed that afternoon.

They described the figure of the familiar, which appeared basically as the rumors said, yet completely changed for the worse. They told me about the homeless children who were living in the crumbling hut. And they recounted the familiar's mysterious actions and how it only showed mercy to the children, leaving without taking a single bite of food for itself.

Sheila and Miss Fran, who had witnessed the whole thing from beginning to end, told me that, ultimately, they had totally lost any inclination to capture the familiar.

"We were supposed to hunt down a familiar that was destroying crops and causing panic among the people. We witnessed no such behavior from the familiar we saw earlier. I can't help but doubt that the familiar we saw is actually a threat to the people at all. Do you know anything about it, Elaina?" Miss Fran looked at me.

I do know.
I know because I got Karen to tell me about her familiar's original form.
I know why the familiar is gathering bread and leaving it at the hut.
I know everything.
"……"
Hesitantly, I opened my mouth.
"Karen's familiar's name is Scieszka."
I told them the story of the familiar and Karen.
I told them a tale of two girls.

The two of them first met when Karen was walking down a back alley by herself.

Scieszka was near death.

Her black hair was tied up in a single ponytail on the back of her head. Her eyes were green. Her skin was a little darker than Karen's, and she had bruises and cuts all over. Her clothes were tattered, and Karen actually couldn't tell whether they were just worn, or if they had been torn apart by whatever had caused her injuries. It looked like she wasn't even wearing clothes at all and was just wrapped in plain cloth.

Right away, Karen could tell that Scieszka was in no condition to walk on her own.

But Karen was still an inexperienced magic user.

She didn't know any spells to heal Scieszka's injuries.

"…Wait here, I'll call someone!" Karen called out to the girl whose name she didn't even know.

At the time, that was about all she could do to help.

"Don't." Scieszka grabbed her hand and stopped her. "It's no use."

According to Scieszka…

She had been beaten by the owner of a bakery. She had stolen some of the bread lined up on a shelf at the shop, been chased into the alley, gotten caught, and taken a beating.

"I always steal from there, see, so I think that I hit the limits of the baker's patience. As he was beating me, he said he was going to make it so I never stole from there again. I'm paying for my own mistakes, you know." The girl grinned foolishly, still stretched out on her side.

For someone who was nearly dead, she somehow seemed to have enough strength left to smile.

"……" Karen looked down at Scieszka. "So then, is there anything I can do?" she asked.

Scieszka answered, "I guess I'd like to eat some bread."

That was her only request.

"……"

Karen wondered what her mother would do in such a situation.

She probably wouldn't hesitate to help.

She decided that if her mother had been there, she would have answered the request with a smile.

"Got it. All right, I'll go buy some bread."

So Karen heeded Scieszka's wishes.

That was the first time Karen had ever eaten bread sold from a bakery in the city.

She didn't think it was particularly tasty. It was hard, and cold, and not really special. She felt that the bread her mother made for her was much better.

But she figured it must taste good to the city folks, because Scieszka devoured the bread with gusto, weeping as she ate.

Mysteriously, Karen and Scieszka seemed to be linked by fate. After that day, every time she went into town, Karen would encounter Scieszka.

One time, Scieszka was being chased by someone. Another time, Scieszka was walking along eating some bread that she had probably stolen. Yet another time, she was gazing into a bakery window with a look of determination in her eyes. Scieszka apparently wandered here and there around the city at all hours of the day and night, and every time Karen saw her, she spoke to her.

"Come to think of it, I haven't thanked you yet, have I?"

One day, Scieszka pressed a bundle into Karen's hands. It was soft and a little warm.

Inside was a single piece of cheap bread.

"Thank you for what you did before. You saved me."

Apparently Scieszka really liked bread. And she must have thought that Karen also liked what she liked.

But...

"...This isn't stolen, is it?"

"That's confidential." Scieszka held a finger up to her lips and smiled.

"What does *confidential* mean?"

"It means I'll tell you once we're better friends."

"But it's obvious, even if you don't try to hide it."

Scieszka had been beaten nearly to death, and yet Karen had seen her stealing from bakeries many times since then. At this stage, even if Scieszka wouldn't admit it, Karen knew perfectly well where the bread she had been handed had come from.

She wasn't happy to be given stolen goods. Even less so if Scieszka had put her life in danger to steal it, as she had before.

"Why do you steal things?"

Karen couldn't understand why. She wondered how on earth Scieszka could cause such trouble for other people and then be so calm about it.

"Why? Because I have no other way to get things. Someone like me can't get a proper job. I can't even feed myself tomorrow. So I've got no choice but to go digging through garbage or steal in order to survive."

Scieszka didn't look pessimistic.

Still speaking in a very cheerful tone of voice, she said, "I don't have any other means of getting by, you know."

Then Scieszka added, "But I'm not unhappy," and turned to look at Karen. "I think it's boring to live life feeling sorry for yourself."

Karen felt like Scieszka had been making fun of her, in a roundabout way, for leading a boring life. Though she knew that Scieszka had no way of knowing the kind of treatment she received at home, she still felt a little bitter about it.

About the fact that she was leading a boring life, trapped on a limited estate, and about the girl who smiled happily despite living as a thief with no family.

After that...

Karen began to take her magical training very seriously. Under her grandmother's instruction, she kept practicing her spells.

Of course, she also kept meeting up with Scieszka whenever she went into town.

Scieszka taught Karen all kinds of things. Like which restaurants threw away the tastiest foods, and how to steal bread from a bakery, and how to pickpocket.

Most of this was not knowledge that Karen needed, but Scieszka talked about it unprompted, in one-sided conversations.

One day, Karen said to Scieszka somewhat cynically, "For someone who refused to answer whether or not that bread was stolen, you sure talk a lot."

With a composed face, as always, Scieszka answered simply, "Didn't I say I would tell you once we were good friends?"

Then she added, "Though I guess you could say I dodged the question because I wanted to become better friends. Nothing gets people invested like a juicy secret," she said.

The two girls did become friends.

Spring, summer, autumn, winter—before long, Scieszka and Karen would chat excitedly whenever they saw each other.

Scieszka was a mysterious girl. She lived a very hard life, after all. With no one by her side, she lived each day not knowing if it would be her last.

She should have been anxious, insecure.

And yet she was always smiling.

"I'll introduce you. This is my house."

One day, Scieszka took Karen to the ruins of a factory and showed her a little hut that had been built out of random scraps of wood. Bits of cloth were spread out over the roof so that the rain wouldn't get into the hut, and similarly, a sheet hung over the entrance.

It was quite a bit smaller than Karen's bedroom. Too small for someone to live in.

That was what Scieszka called home.

"...It doesn't look like a house."

"You're supposed to say, 'Wow, what a great house!' Even if you don't mean it, you know." Scieszka puffed up her cheeks and opened the cloth curtain. "I've got a family, too."

Several little girls were sitting inside. The girls, who all looked a lot like Scieszka, were gathered around a book propped open on a wooden plank, reading.

When they lifted their gaunt faces, they all smiled.

"Welcome home, big sister!"

"Welcome back!"

"No food yet?"

As soon as she saw them, Karen understood.

She knew that the girls in the hut were children with no families, just like Scieszka.

That was when Karen first realized that there were many more children in the same circumstances as Scieszka.

And that Scieszka had been giving the stolen bread and other food to girls younger than herself.

"Big sister, how do you read this word?" one of the girls asked, holding the book up and pointing to it. Scieszka hummed for a minute, staring at the book, but she had probably never learned to read and write.

"Sorry, your big sister's a dummy. I have no idea," she answered with a smile.

"Useless!"

"Totally!"

Scieszka's sisters teased her.

"Come on, now!" She smiled, as always.

"I have a dream, you know."

The second spring had arrived since the two girls had met.

Munching on stolen bread, Scieszka tore a piece off and pushed it into Karen's hands as she said, "I dream of saving up lots of money and leaving the city when I'm grown, to run a bakery in some distant land."

Karen, holding the bread she had been given, asked, "Have you ever made it before? Bread, that is."

"Of course I haven't. But I've already decided on the name of my shop."

"…What will it be?"

"The Black Bakery."

"…What's the inspiration for the name?"

"My hair is black."

"That's too obvious."

"…Ah, wait. Not that…how about The Black and Gold Bakery?"

"…And I suppose I'll be working there?"

"Not just you, Karen. I'll hire the girls who live with me, too, and the five of us will somehow manage to run the place. And…," she continued, "after we get that going, I want those girls to live decent lives. I don't want them to have to go through what I've been through. I want them to live honestly, without stealing. I've suffered enough, and there's no need for those girls to suffer the same. So I want to save up money as quickly as I can and get out of here," she said.

"……"

Karen marveled at Scieszka.

She was always amazed by her friend.

"Why are you telling me all this?"

Scieszka had told Karen every little thing about herself, like how she lived her life, and what kind of family she lived with, and about her dreams.

Karen wondered why she had done that.

"You have the same eyes as I do," Scieszka answered casually, as if it was the most obvious thing.

"What kind of eyes?"

"Eyes that want to escape from this place as soon as possible."

Scieszka's eyes were clear as she spoke.

Karen looked away from Scieszka, as if to escape, and bit into her bread.

"This is terrible."

"You're supposed to say it's delicious, even if you don't mean it."

Before long, Karen began visiting Scieszka's house frequently. She had lots of books in her mansion, and she could read and write.

She started to help the little girls with their studies.

The days went by peacefully.

Ever since Karen had started going out into the city alone, her magic had improved day by day.

"Perfect. I have nothing left to teach you," her grandmother told her one day.

That year, it was officially decided that Karen would be granted a familiar on her fourteenth birthday.

Scieszka was invited to the estate on the day of Karen's fourteenth birthday.

"Your magic has improved, thanks to your friend, right? In that case, we need to thank her, as a family."

Karen's mother was delighted and suggested the idea of bringing Scieszka to the house.

Karen honestly felt a little reluctant at the thought of bringing Scieszka around. Her family's mansion was obviously very luxurious, while Scieszka lived her life not knowing where or when she'd get her next meal.

Karen wondered what she would do if Scieszka's visit made her feel inferior—or made her hate Karen.

So she was hesitant.

But Scieszka was always so cheerful in front of Karen.

After wavering for a while, Karen finally invited Scieszka to her home.

"...It doesn't look like a house."

Scieszka, looking shabby as always, stood in front of the gate, staring up at the mansion with her mouth hanging open.

When Karen showed her inside, the servants, along with Karen's parents and grandmother, came out to greet the two girls.

Everyone who came out of the house to greet them stared at Scieszka, aghast. Probably because she was such a shabby little girl. They probably couldn't believe that such a dirty child was Karen's friend.

So Karen puffed out her chest. "This girl is my friend, Scieszka," she said clearly. "The fact that I learned to use magic is all thanks to her."

Karen's grandmother let out a sigh, and the servants were obviously flustered. It was not surprising that everyone was so perplexed, since the two friends were so different in social standing.

Only one person smiled tenderly at the two girls.

"I see—so you are Karen's friend?"

It was Karen's mother. "You're the one who's been looking after my daughter, are you? Thank you. I hope you enjoy your time here today."

Karen's mother welcomed Scieszka as an honored guest.

Scieszka seemed hungry, so she fed her a delicious meal. Scieszka was dirty, so she let her take a bath. Scieszka was wearing tattered clothes, so she dressed her in the finest outfit that they had. By that afternoon, Scieszka fit right in on the estate. She was dressed in beautiful clothes and decorated with beautiful accessories. She looked just like she had lived there all along.

"Amazing...I look like a different person."

Scieszka's reflection in the mirror looked like someone else entirely.

"You can keep those clothes," Karen's mother said, placing one hand on Scieszka's shoulder. "Take good care of them."

"Such nice clothes, is it really okay...for me to have them?"

"Yes. It's no problem. They're extras anyway, and besides...," Karen's mother continued, "...you're Karen's friend, which makes you family."

In Karen's family, children were treated as fully grown from the day that they were granted their own familiar.

On the day of Karen's fourteenth birthday, as the sun set, all of her family gathered in one room of the mansion, including the servants and the familiars.

Scieszka was instructed to stand beside Karen's mother and grandmother.

"......"

But the strange thing was that one essential party was missing—the animal that was to become Karen's familiar.

Karen had assumed that she would be using a mouse or something, just like she did during practice. She had been under the impression that she would be employing some animal or other as her familiar.

But there was no animal on the altar.

"Mother?" Karen had never learned how to produce a familiar from nothing. "What about the animal...?"

She gazed at her mother with eyes full of anxiety.

Her mother smiled at her tenderly as always.

"It's right here."

Karen didn't understand.

There is no animal anywhere. The only familiars here are already bound by master-servant compacts; otherwise it's just people.

"Right here," her mother said.

Standing beside her, Karen's friend Scieszka just watched the two of them, oblivious to what was going on.

"This girl will become your familiar."

Then there was a spray of red.

It fell from Scieszka's neck, onto the floor. Karen's mother was holding a short knife. When Scieszka let out a mute scream and collapsed, the mother stepped over the fallen girl and approached Karen.

Then she whispered into her ear, "All right, Karen. Try casting the spell, just like Grandma taught you."

Karen was astonished. She struggled to make sense of what had taken place. It was like the inside of her mind was blank.

Her mother spoke to her as gently as always. "We were surprised when you brought her here, but I won't deny you. It's fine. If this girl is important to you, I'm sure you'll be successful."

"Mo...ther...?"

"Come now. Hurry. If you don't do it quickly, she'll die. If you turn her into your familiar, the wound will heal. If you don't want her to die, hurry and make her into your familiar."

Karen looked down and saw Scieszka.

She saw Scieszka, suffering on the cold floor, spitting up blood.

"Scieszka..."

She called her friend's name.

"Come now, hurry." Karen's mother took her hand and pointed her wand toward Scieszka. "Cast the spell quickly. It's all right. You can do it, just as I once did. I know you'll do a fine job."

Scieszka's pretty clothes were dirty now. They were covered in blood, tears, and saliva.

Karen had never questioned the customs of her family. She had never worried about where they had gotten generations of familiars, or what forms they had held before the ritual.

Finally, she realized how foolish she had been.

"Ah..."

She realized her own foolishness after it was too late to turn back, no matter how much she regretted it.

With a trembling hand, Karen readied her wand. With an endless stream of tears, through a blurred vision, sobbing inconsolably, she took aim.

"Aaah…! Aaaaaaaaah!"
Cursing herself for her own ignorance, she cast the spell.

That day, Karen became a fully realized mage of her family.
In the puddle of blood on the floor was her familiar, which had taken the shape of a black wolf.
"Great job, Karen! It was a success! Have a look! It's a great familiar, isn't it?"
"……"
Karen's mother stroked her head happily.
Karen lay flat on the floor and apologized over and over and over and over again.
For bringing Scieszka to a place like this. For stealing any chance of her dream ever coming true. For the fact that she would no longer be able to help the little girls grow into splendid adults.
She kept on apologizing to the wolf.
Resentment toward her family coursed through her veins.
She hated them—her grandmother, who believed that employing familiars was the only correct way to live, and her mother, who had never actually had the least bit of kindness in her. From the bottom of her heart, Karen wished to escape from that place as soon as possible.
From the bottom of her heart, she wished that everything and everyone would disappear.
Just then…
The black wolf bit into her mother's neck.
"Wha—!"
Its powerful jaws tightened around her throat, gouging into her flesh so that she couldn't even scream. It kept biting, until her expression was twisted with fear.
"You beast—!"
While everyone else was too astonished to move, Karen's grandmother readied her wand.
"Hey, Karen!" She glared at the girl. "Stop that anima—"

But before she could finish, the wolf bit into her arm.

"Aaaaaah! Aaah! What have you done!"

What happened next was like a scene from hell.

Karen's mother stood up, bleeding, and fired off a spell—a blade of force slashed at Scieszka's leg. A brown wolf bit into Scieszka's throat, but Scieszka did the same and tore at the throat of Karen's mother's familiar. Covered in blood, the two of them rolled around in the middle of the room. Karen's grandmother tried to restrain them from afar, but Scieszka must have seen her and bit her in the leg. The old woman's face warped with intense pain, and she lashed out at Scieszka, but every time she landed a hit, Scieszka dug her fangs in more and more powerfully, rending the flesh.

The first to die was Karen's mother. Next was her grandmother, then all the servants who were running around trying to escape. No one made it out alive.

"Ah...ahh..."

In the middle of the room, surrounded by screams and the spray of blood, stood Karen, hanging her head and sobbing.

Eventually, once all the noise had died down, she dared to look up.

Her surroundings were soaked in blood.

Gradually, she realized that her spell had succeeded. The pact with her familiar had definitely taken hold. But her intense emotions had sent her familiar on a rampage.

The gruesome scene before her eyes was the result.

"......"

She wondered what Scieszka was thinking, now that the rampage was over and she had come back to herself, looking at the sea of blood spreading out before her. Scieszka surveyed her surroundings with her lovely green eyes and let out one frail cry, then bounded for the exit of the mansion, dragging her leg behind her.

"Wait. Scieszka. Please, wait!"

Karen sank to the floor in a daze and called her name.

But she didn't know what to say to get Scieszka to come back. She had turned her friend into a monster, and made her kill people, and didn't know what she could possibly say after that.

In the end, she said nothing at all.

Karen's familiar disappeared into the dark of night without looking back.

○

After the tragic incident, half a year went by, but there was nothing that Karen could do on her own. She just hung her head, powerless, and didn't accomplish a thing.

She knew that she had to turn Scieszka back into a human as soon as she possibly could.

But her distress addled her wits, and as a result, all her potions were failures, and all she did was destroy her house, without anything to show for it.

But that was because she had been going up against the problem alone.

"First of all, I'll be staying here in the mansion twenty-four-seven, starting today. So let's hurry up and make that potion."

It was the day after I'd reported the situation to Miss Fran and Sheila.

I headed for the estate as the sun rose and began researching potions right away. Karen looked like she hadn't slept, and she stared at me with an expression so hollow, I couldn't tell whether she was awake or asleep. "…Thanks," she murmured. It was an automatic reaction.

Just how long has it been since this girl slept?

"You ought to go rest for a while," I suggested.

"No." For someone who was just barely conscious, she managed to respond very clearly when she was refusing me. "I'd rather research than sleep."

"Um, in your condition, you'd be better off sleeping rather than conducting research."

"No. I'd rather research than sleep."

"......"

"I'd rather research than sleep."

When she spoke the same words like a broken record, I gave up and let out a sigh.

The two of us took our work very seriously. Karen would write the recipe for a potion, then I would mix it. The work was perfectly divided. Though I also did my own research on familiars while Karen was puzzling over her recipes.

"...What do you think of the compound in this recipe?"

"I'll try mixing it." I skimmed over the recipe Karen handed me and then mixed a batch. "Finished...and it's a shrinking potion."

"Hmm," Karen thought. "...It won't return a familiar to normal but maybe we can use it."

No, no.

"Also, as a side effect, anyone who drinks this will have their lifespan shortened by about one hundred years."

"Wouldn't that mean instant death?"

"This one's a bust."

But she wasn't discouraged, and before long, Karen brought me another recipe.

"How about this one?"

"I see, let's try it." I mixed that one as well. "Done. This is a potion that can create an inexhaustible supply of gold."

"Got it. Useless."

Karen tossed the liquid aside.

"Ah...um, sure it is...yes."

Every day, I kept mixing and mixing, and kept shaking my head no, no.

"This one's perfect, huh?" I held up a piece of paper that contained an ordinary cooking recipe.

"Look at this. I made a recipe." Karen proudly brought me a blank sheet of paper.

Such outrageous things did happen sometimes, maybe because we were exhausted, but even so, we continued the work.

For one, two, three, four days we continued the work, on and on.

Morning, noon, and night we went on endlessly mixing magic potions that all turned out to be failures.

And then finally...

After suffering through failure after failure, drifting through the days like a dream, or perhaps a waking nightmare...

...Finally we saw the light.

It happened on the fifth day of our work together at Karen's house.

"Look at this."

I understood immediately what kind of effect the potion would have.

I started mixing the potion right away. I followed the recipe, assembled the ingredients, threw them into a cauldron, infused them with magic, and stirred as the mixture simmered.

Karen fell asleep while I was working, so I did every bit of the job by myself. But there was no helping that. After all, I was tasting only a tiny bit of the suffering she had gone through long before I had arrived.

It's good for her to have some time to sleep soundly.

"Rest well, Karen."

I put a blanket over her shoulders and let her sleep, facedown on her desk.

Scattered all around her were finished potions.

●

Day one.

Looking down from high overhead, I clearly recognized Scieszka's usual behavior. Every day, she dropped down from the rooftops into town and went rummaging through the garbage or stole some food. She was living the same way she always had before.

Her appearance had changed, yet her actions were the same.

She stole things and provided food for the girls waiting in the hut, but she rarely ate anything herself and just wandered from place to place.

That was how she passed the days.

She didn't know who she was, and no one knew her. She was just a monster, and she lived like that for half a year.

Alone.

Never meeting anyone face-to-face.

"......"

But those days were over.

Scieszka was walking around town when she came upon a piece of bread sitting on a plate. The girl who had been turned into a black wolf sniffed the bread gently, then picked it up in her mouth and started walking. After she had gone a little farther, there was another piece of bread sitting on a plate. There was also a bag sitting beside it.

Clearly, this was very suspicious. It was an obvious trap.

Even so, Scieszka picked up the bread and stepped forward on frail legs, placing both pieces into the bag. She must have been thinking about providing the girls with bread again.

As I watched from high up in the air, Scieszka wandered on and on, picking up the pieces of bread that were laid out like guideposts on the road and packing them into the bag.

And then she stepped forward.

To the last piece of bread.

She stopped under a lamppost.

"......"

Scieszka looked up.

There was a girl there.

"Scieszka."

Her golden hair went down past her shoulders, and her robe was elaborately decorated all over, and seemed very, very expensive. She looked like the daughter of a noble family. She was probably about fourteen years old, and there was still youth in her features.

When she kneeled before the eyes of the black wolf, she finally broke.

"I'm so sorry I hurt you…," she said tearfully.

Karen, the familiar's mistress, was crying.

The black wolf didn't answer. She just squinted at Karen.

Finally, Karen embraced Scieszka. As she stroked the stiff, fluffy black fur, she cried and smiled and addressed her friend.

"Let me take responsibility. For the rest of our lives, for a long, long time to come, let me make amends for your loneliness…," Karen said.

In her hand, she held a small vial—the magic potion that had only just been perfected the day before.

And then…

As Sheila and I, along with Elaina, watched from the sky, Karen administered the potion to Scieszka.

Day one.

The first day after completion of the potion.

Their long, long days of loneliness came to an end.

○

It was very difficult for us to summarize everything that had happened, but we managed to convey it all to the government official, without keeping anything secret.

We explained that Karen's familiar was a girl—that it was Scieszka. And that Scieszka certainly hadn't been rampaging around town. We also explained that Karen had not just shut herself away out of grief.

We told the government official that the familiar would never terrorize the town again.

We laid everything out in clear detail.

"…I see. It's difficult to believe, hearing that all so suddenly, but—"

But it's the truth.

Since three witches are each giving you the same testimony, it would be troublesome if you didn't believe us.

After she'd finished interviewing us, the official told us she was going to talk with Karen. Probably to confirm the facts.

The rest would be decided by the people of the city. In the end, we were outsiders, and wouldn't have anything more to do with the matter.

Besides, it wasn't difficult to imagine how things were going to go for the two girls, even without our involvement.

If I had one concern, it was that there was basically nothing of value left in Karen's ransacked house. It seemed like it would be very difficult for her to lead a normal life like that.

"By the way, I have one more request..." I tilted my head as I pocketed only a few of the gold coins that the official had offered me in payment.

"...What is it?" The official also tilted her head and frowned, looking puzzled.

"I want you to give the rest to Karen."

"......"

The official didn't say anything for a while.

Maybe she was having trouble understanding what I was doing. Or maybe she was stunned because the two people beside me had also done the same thing.

But eventually, the official nodded. "...Understood. If that's what you ladies want."

Then she collected the three stacks of coins sitting on the table.

After we had divulged everything to the government official, we left the city immediately.

There was no need for us to stay any longer, and Miss Fran was in the middle of her own return trip.

If anything, I already felt bad that we had stayed in a single city for almost a week. The fact that it took me so much time to mix the potion was to blame.

"Are you two headed for the harbor now?" Sheila cocked her head.

We were standing in front of the city gates. Sheila was holding her pipe in her mouth as always, but the wind was blowing and the smoke curled up into the sky, so the smell didn't bother me that much.

Miss Fran nodded at her. "That's right. That's my plan. What are you doing?" she asked.

Sheila made a slightly bitter expression. "I've got another job to get to. Guess this is where we part ways."

"Oh, that's too bad," Miss Fran said quite readily, in spite of the actual words. "I can tell that you're enthusiastic about your work, but don't push yourself too hard, okay?"

"Does it seem like I am?"

"I was just being polite."

"……" Sheila shrugged. "I'm jealous of you two. If I had my way, I'd like to fly over to the harbor, too, but…work is work. Unfortunately, I can't go with you." She already looked fairly exhausted. "You don't need to see me off. It's not like this is our final farewell, or anything."

"We'll meet again someday, so don't feel like you have to come with us." Miss Fran smiled.

Sheila sucked in a breath, exhaled, and blew out smoke like a sigh. "It's such a pain the way your responsibilities increase as you get older. You can't even do what you want anymore. I'd like to go with you, but I can't."

Sheila had been working at the United Magic Association for a long time and probably had a lot of responsibility there.

She had the duty of going from place to place and resolving incidents as an Association-affiliated witch.

She had the duty of teaching classes as a professor.

She had the duty of being Saya's teacher.

"……" Miss Fran was a little bewildered. "Um, I'm not sure how to respond, now that you've said something like that so suddenly…"

"……" Sheila chuckled at seeing Fran that way. "Well, enjoy your two-person journey as much as possible. The third wheel is leaving now."

And then, without any further parting words, Sheila turned on her heel and walked off.

Though she kept her back to us, we could see ribbons of smoke wafting from her silhouette, and an odor that made me screw up my face in disgust was carried our way by the breeze.

We also turned our backs on Sheila.

Neither of us suggested getting on our brooms.

We just started slowly walking.

I turned to look at Miss Fran. "I wonder what kind of place is waiting for us next?"

She looked at me and gave a vague answer. "I bet it'll be a place fairly close to the seashore, where the scent of the ocean fills the air."

But right after that, she added with a smile, "I hope it's someplace wonderful."

I just said, "Me too," and nodded, then kept walking alongside my teacher as always.

Before long, the smell of smoke that made me screw up my face had dissipated. Without turning around, Miss Fran and I pulled out our brooms and set off.

Toward the end of our journey together.

CHAPTER 6

A Country Girl, a History Addict, and the Aroma of Wheat

Linaria's history hunt continued.

Since the whole period from late winter through early spring was a holiday, neither of us was too concerned with the return trip. Far from it. We told each other optimistically that no matter how far we got from Latorita, we could just head back when the holidays were drawing to a close. But we ended up traveling for so long in this cheerful state of mind that I wondered whether we might really have gone too far to make it back by the end of the holiday, no matter how hard we might try.

Still, we weren't worried.

Our first priority was to enjoy the present, not worry about the future.

"Looks like there's a little city there if we go just a bit farther this way," Linaria said, sitting atop her broom with the map spread out in front of her.

"What kind of place is it?"

At my inquiry, Linaria closed the map suddenly and answered, "There's no further information."

Oh-hoh, I see!

Which means…

"So we can look forward to finding out once we get there?"

Linaria just smiled at my words. "We sure can."

○

Immediately after we'd passed through the city gates, I said confidently, "Oh, this is definitely a good city, no doubt about it!"

Right next to the gates, in the best possible place to attract hungry travelers, there was a small shop with an incredible aroma wafting out of it.

The place wasn't obviously flourishing, but neither did it seem to be in decline. Sending out another wave of that wonderful fragrance, the baker, who had apparently been on the watch for customers, opened the door and waited for us to come in.

Three girls with smiles on their faces stood in front of the shop, shouting, "Fresh-baked bread!" and "It's delicious!" and so on.

At first glance, I could see that this was a lively city.

"Miss, are you a traveler? If you like, how about trying some of our bread?"

One of the girls, holding a basket filled with lots of fresh-baked loaves, pressed one into my hand.

Oh, what?

"Um, ah, I don't have much money to spare right now..."

"That's fine. I'll give you one for free."

The girl pushed more insistently.

Huh? For free? Is that for real? Hooray!

Completely captivated by the delicious smell, I took a bite of the bread.

"Ah...so good..."

The flavor of the bread, soft and warm like sunlight, spread through my mouth. It felt like flowers were blooming all around me. It was just my imagination, but that's what it felt like eating the bread. I was filled with joy.

"Linaria! This is so good! It's incredible! Try some—here!"

I vigorously pushed a bit of the bread into Linaria's hands, but she tilted her head quizzically.

"Incredible, you say? Then shall we go buy some of each type?"

Contrary to my wild excitement, Linaria's response was extremely dry. There was even a slight air of condescension.

Who are you, my mother...?

As I munched on the rest of the free bread, I started walking, with Linaria following behind me. Seeing as how I worked part-time at a bakery, we could kill two birds with one stone and scope out the competition by getting some of each type of bread in the store and eating every last bit. Filled with energy, I headed for the store.

And the bakery welcomed us.

"Oh-hoh!"

Well, well.

The bakery was very clean inside, and the place had obviously just opened recently.

Two women stood on the other side of the counter, smiles on their faces just like the girls outside, and they greeted me and Linaria when we entered, "Welcome!"

One was a lovely young woman with blond hair that went down about to her shoulders. She had a refined look to her. She appeared to be in her mid-twenties.

Next to her was a young woman with black hair and dark skin. She appeared to be about the same age as the blonde, and at a glance, she seemed like a lively character.

The two women appeared to be running the place.

"Hello."

After bowing slightly to the two of them, I strolled around the inside of the shop.

In a quiet city, in a peaceful shop, Linaria and I enjoyed a little break, in a bakery run by two women who seemed tremendously happy.

The shop's name was The Black and Gold and Gray Bakery.

When I asked the two proprietors what the name meant, they looked at each other and smiled roguishly.

"It's confidential."

Afterword

"Mister Shiraishi...starting today, your teeth are going to hurt, and you probably won't be able to eat anything, so please prepare yourself for that, all right?"

If the alignment of your teeth isn't an absolute disaster, then whenever you mention your distress or discuss your plans to have them fixed, people around you actually question it, like, "Huh? Are your teeth really that bad?" That's about how mine were.

But struggles with your body are a very personal sort of thing, hard for other people to understand. So at age twenty-five, I finally got around to fixing the misaligned teeth that had been troubling me since middle school. Those words up there were what the dentist said to me when I went in for the procedure.

And I said, "Ha-ha-ha! I'll be fine! I'm stronger than the pain, you know!"

My words were filled with an unearned confidence. Maybe it was because the dentist I had been going to—Y Dental—was an extremely conscientious clinic that had recently acquired some new equipment. Maybe it was because every procedure I'd had to date had gone very smoothly. Whatever the reason, I placed tremendous confidence in the orthodontic prowess of Y Dental.

And, in fact, the installation of my braces went extremely well, without any pain at all. Before I knew it, the dentist had finished attaching them, and I left the clinic in an extremely good mood.

"Ha-ha-ha! I knew this would be no big deal!"

Just before I got out the door…

"Please don't eat anything too tough, starting today, okay?"

The dentist gave me that advice, which I immediately, completely forgot.

That evening—

"...I've finally gotten the braces I wanted for so long, so I ought to have a big celebration tonight, right?"

I said something intensely idiotic like that and rushed into a nearby restaurant. I ordered a fried pork cutlet. Promising myself that I would do my best to fix my teeth, starting that day, I ate the cutlet that was set down in front of me.

Why, this doesn't hurt at all; what was I scared of? Heh-heh-heh-heh! I was totally calm and collected.

But the more I chewed, and the more time passed, the more my teeth gradually began to scream from the pressure of the braces and the force of my jaw chewing the meat.

And then, once I was done eating a small slice of pork cutlet—

"Ah........................this hurts like crazy...................................!"

I set down my chopsticks.

In the corner of the restaurant, at the booth by the window, there was a twenty-five-year-old man pressing his hand against his mouth and shaking. To all appearances, he probably looked like a man who had gone out into the world and had the first hot meal of his life. But actually, he was just a pitiful, unlucky man who was seriously on the verge of tears despite his age, just because his teeth hurt.

I decided I would listen carefully to everything my dentist said from then on...

Anyway, leaving such stories aside, before I get to the proper Afterword, I'll give some comments on each chapter. Anyone who wants to avoid spoilers, skip forward a few pages, please!

- Chapter 1   The Giants' Kitchen

The original sources of inspiration for this story were *Gulliver's Travels* and "The Restaurant of Many Orders." I'd been wanting to write a short story based on "The Restaurant of Many Orders" for some time, but since our main character is allergic to cats, the only outcome I could see was her refusing to go into the restaurant at all. "Huh? I'm not going into a suspicious place like that!" So I rejected the idea for a long time, but by Volume 9, one way or another it came out as a restaurant run by tiny little women. Personally, I like the captain best.

- Chapter 2   A Country Girl, a History Addict, and a Potion Dosing

This is Alte and Linaria's second appearance. I had fun writing dialogue for the Alte and Linaria that I remembered so fondly. Originally I was planning to have Priscilla and crew appear in a "Wandering Through Time" chapter in Volume 7, but much to my chagrin, we had to cut that one for length, so I was happy to be able to fit it in now.

- Chapter 3   The Resurrection Lily That Blooms in Solitude

I have a strong emotional attachment to the resurrection lily. It was possibly the first flower that I ever thought was beautiful. I decided that if I ever put a resurrection lily in one of my books, I would have it show up in a symbolic story, and I held on to that idea for a long time. By the way, resurrection lilies are often seen blooming alone in the countryside, and apparently that's because they're grown as mole repellents. That is to say, more so than the multicolored blossoms lining florist shops, I saw a flower that was just quietly carrying out its task and thought it was beautiful. What's up with that?

The definitions of serial killers that Sheila alludes to in the chapter are based on the serial killer classifications that the FBI uses to sort them into systematic-nonsystematic types. This is a fantasy series, so I changed it a bit, though.

By the way, in flower language, the resurrection lily signifies, among other things, "passion, isolation, reunion, resignation, and sad memories."

- Chapter 4   Cinderella

I intended to make this a crisp, short comedy chapter, but as I was finishing it up, I realized that it had become quite long. I think it's because once I decided to write a story on the theme of Cinderella, there were lots of points that I had to be sure to touch on...

I realized that once I'm done writing them, the princes that appear in this series have a really high chance of turning out stupid.

- Chapter 5   Familiars

This is a bit of insider information, but when *Journey of Elaina* was optioned for commercial publishing, my editor floated the idea of giving the witches familiars, but I rejected the idea out of hand. "No way! Absolutely not!" I didn't remember this until I was in the middle of writing this chapter, not until I had reached Volume 9 of the series, but now, finally, a familiar has made its first appearance. This is similar to what happened with Chapter 1 of Volume 9—actually there are quite a lot of stories on subjects that get pushed back due to various considerations, like the balance of each volume as a whole.

Take your best guess as to why Karen didn't have a father.

- Chapter 6   A Country Girl, a History Addict, and the Aroma of Wheat

I tried to split the time line within one story, as I did in Volume 3 with "The Wall That Travelers Inscribe." I didn't have enough time, and tried rearranging it in every which way, but I'm glad that I was finally able to arrive at this punch line.

This book is a continuation of Volume 8, with Elaina and Miss Fran traveling together.

I haven't written the manuscript for Volume 10 yet (actually, I'm sure you could have guessed that), but in Volume 10, I'm planning for Elaina's journey with Miss Fran to come to an end. Timing-wise, there was no other place where we could put Chapter 3, "The Resurrection Lily That Blooms in Solitude," so this book ended up having a lot of longer chapters.

The next book is going to be a Limited Special Edition with a drama CD included (preorders are open now!), so that's one more reason why I'm glad that I could write some stories in Volume 9 that will continue into the next book. I don't have any plans to conclude the series with

Volume 10, but it would make me very happy if you would stick with me at least until the end of Miss Fran and Elaina's tandem journey.

Now then, on to the acknowledgments.

To M, the head editor: When we first met, you were kind enough to be concerned for me. "You don't eat much, do you?" you asked. Now that I've gotten braces installed, I'm back to being Jougi Shiraishi, who doesn't eat. Moving forward, I'd like to become Jougi Shiraishi, who appreciates quality over quantity in food, and I'd just like to say it makes me very happy that you've stuck with me for so long.

To Azure: Thank you for your work on the illustrations, as always. Your illustrations for the Amazon limited edition of Volume 9 are really preposterously lovely, and a primo work of art. The moment they arrived, I decided to keep them as family heirlooms.

To Ikki Nanao: I'm really enjoying all the updates in the comicalized version of *Journey of Elaina*. I've already said this many times on Twitter and my other social media accounts, but your original plot twists in Book 2 were just the best...

To everyone involved with these books, everyone at SB Creative, everyone in distribution, all the bookstore employees, and everyone who had a part in the publication of this book: Thank you all very much. And thank you in advance for next time.

To all my readers: Thank you so much for sticking with me through Volume 9. Volume 10, as well as the Limited Special Edition with drama CD, should go on sale simultaneously around mid-August. Thank you so much for your support!

That's all I have to say, but between when I got my braces and the time I'm writing this now, my body weight has dropped by about ten kilograms.

I wasn't really all that fat to begin with, but after I got the braces, I was surviving on porridge and energy jelly every day, so my weight took a sudden dive like the Black Monday stock market, and now I'm below average. It's pretty bad.

The pain in my teeth has finally let up, and I'm back to being able to eat again, but it doesn't seem like the size of my stomach has gone back to normal, which has improved my undisciplined eating habits. Thanks to that, my treadmill can take a little break.

I hope that, even as my weight declines, the popularity of the *Journey of Elaina* series only continues to grow from here. Well then, let's meet here again in August, shall we? See you then!